Relative Danger

'Jon, it's only your father, not King Kong. Why do you . . .?'

'Look, you don't know him. I don't know him either, come to that. But you wouldn't like him, I guarantee it. Even *you* couldn't find something nice to say about him.'

On holiday with his long-estranged and rather moody father, Jon quickly finds they have little in common and even less to talk about. Boredom sets in. Then he sees Casey.

From the start he likes her looks—but what is she really like? How can he get to know her? Jon's chance comes when a strange and chilling chain of events unexpectedly throws the two of them together.

JANICE BROWN lives with her husband and three children in Scotland. A former teacher, she now divides her time between writing, bringing up the family and her favourite recreation, listening to music.

For Ian

Relative Danger

Janice Brown

A LION PAPERBACK
Oxford · Batavia · Sydney

Copyright © 1992 Janice Brown

The author asserts the moral right
to be identified as the author of this work

Published by
Lion Publishing plc
Sandy Lane West, Oxford, England
ISBN 0 7459 2539 1
Albatross Books Pty Ltd
PO Box 320, Sutherland, NSW 2232, Australia
ISBN 0 7324 0604 8

First edition 1992

The characters and situations in this book are entirely imaginary
and bear no relation to any real person or actual happening.

Acknowledgments
My thanks are due to Bill Shorthose whose advice proved
invaluable in the writing of this story

A catalogue record of this book is available
from the British Library

Printed and bound in Great Britain
by Cox & Wyman Ltd, Reading

Contents

1

Fooling around

The first time I saw the girl, she was getting out of a nice-looking red Peugeot. She was carrying a sports bag, and her hair looked wet, so my guess was she'd been swimming. The boy who'd been driving had the same dark hair. Since they didn't walk hand in hand up the path, I thought he might be a brother, not a boyfriend.

I watched the house for a while after that, hoping she'd reappear, but nothing happened. Later on, when my father had finished his unpacking and discovered he had no cigarettes, he sent me out to buy some. I walked down and back on their side of the street, so I'd have to pass the front of their house, but there wasn't any way I could see into it without going up the path.

On the return trip I had a quick look into the car. It was one of the larger Peugeot models, this year's registration. So they weren't poor. Inside it was clean and anonymous, apart from some scraps of silver and purple paper, on the floor at the passenger side, which told me she liked milk chocolate. I preferred plain, but I thought I could adapt.

Their three-storeyed house didn't look as if it had been subdivided, which was in keeping with the car. Most of the rest were, including the one my father had rented for us. I'd never been in Glasgow before and I suppose I was expecting something less sedate. After all, when Glasgow's in the news, it's usually because rival gangs are at each other's throats. So the street surprised me.

It was nice enough to look at—a curving Victorian sandstone terrace with chestnut and lime trees either side—but it didn't seem like the kind of place where anything much ever happened. The far end was blocked off with bollards, so the only people driving in and out were those who lived there, and the last four houses on the north side were some kind of school, deserted for the summer.

When I'd asked my father what we were going to be doing, he'd made noises about showing me the city, the home of his boyhood, just as soon as he got things sorted out. I'd said, 'Fine, that's OK.'

My expectations were not high. I'd felt from the moment we left Norfolk that I'd been dropped into a play where I didn't know what my lines were. I suppose I could have made it easier for him, chatted about the weather or something, but I'm no good at that kind of thing. I mean, why talk, when you've got nothing to say? Although, to be honest, there was plenty I could have said, like where have you been for the last nine years of my life and how come you suddenly remembered you had a son? Those questions were bitter in my mouth more or less all the time, but I kept my lips shut. The strong, silent type.

Apart from that dark-haired girl in the pink T-shirt, nothing else of interest happened on the first day.

The second day, we were supposed to be going somewhere called the Burrell Collection. Old tapestries and Chinese vases. Just my kind of thing. I was killing time staring at nothing happening in the street, when suddenly there she was again, walking along carrying a couple of bulging plastic bags. Her hair was tied back with one of those filmy scarfs, the same shade of bright yellow as her baggy T-shirt. Nothing shy about the colours she wore.

When she reached their gate, she squashed herself through, ducking under a big fuchsia bush that curved over the path. Something fell from one bag. I watched her disappear into the house; and waited for her to miss whatever was in the packet. I watched for at least five minutes. She didn't come out.

My father heard me open the door that led to the landing. He came out of the room he was calling his 'study', the one room in the flat that had a lock.

'Where are you going?'

'Outside. It's stuffy through there.'

'We're going out soon.'

'I thought we were going after lunch.'

'No, we can have lunch there.'

I shrugged my shoulders. It wasn't what he'd said earlier, but it made no difference to me.

'Well, all right,' he conceded. 'But I'm almost finished. Don't wander away.'

I pushed the door. His voice followed me, 'Ten minutes, Jonathan. Be back at quarter to.'

I ran down the two flights, past the shut doors of the other tenants, meeting nobody, through the main door and out. On the far side of the road, the white plastic packet still lay wedged under the metal gate.

It looked like a couple of meat chops. I dusted the wrapper and advanced to the doorbell. There was only one name. Bradley. So my first guess had been right. The whole three floors were theirs. When nobody came in answer to the bell, I thought briefly about trying to push the packet through the letter-box, but then I thought, no, it might tear. Also, they might have a dog, who would get the meat before she did. So I leaned harder on the doorbell.

It seemed like a long time before anything happened. The dark wooden door had a fancy frosted glass panel on the top half, so I could see who was coming, and it wasn't her. Which was a pity, because I'd been wondering if she'd look as good face to face as she had from a distance.

It wasn't the dark-haired boy either. This one was fair, about my height but broader, maybe three or four years older than me.

'Hi. I saw this on your path. I live across the street.'

I held the meat out to him. He looked at me blankly.

Maybe it was my English accent. I tried again, spacing the words.

'The girl with the dark hair. I think she dropped it.'

'Oh. All right. You'd better come in.'

I followed him into the hallway.

'Casey!' he yelled. 'Somebody for you.'

Two things happened almost simultaneously. The dark-haired girl came into sight, swinging round the banister halfway up the stairs. She began to say

10

something but instantly her words were drowned out as a door at the far end of the hall crashed open, and two figures rushed out. The one in front was staggering, clutching at his chest, and the one behind was miming an exaggerated machine-gun attack.

My reflexes were too slow. The one who was under attack crashed sideways into my stomach, knocking me off my feet. The girl's high voice and the lower one of the fair-haired boy mingled in yells of protest as I slammed with a grunt into the half-closed door behind me.

After a few seconds, the boy who'd knocked me down leaned over and caught me by the shoulders. I recognized him as the one who'd been driving the Peugeot. He looked about twenty or so. Straight dark-brown hair and dark eyes.

'Are you all right, kid?' he asked, telling the other one, who was now on his knees, still stuttering insanely like a machine-gun, to shut up.

'Hey, I'm really sorry about that,' he went on. 'Did I hurt you? Mano, would you please give that a rest?'

The gun noises stopped. The boy who'd been making them folded his arms across his chest and stared at the ceiling, with a penitent expression on his face, like an angel gazing up to heaven. He was very tanned, Italian-looking, with short black curls, about the same age as his friend.

As I pulled myself cautiously into a sitting position, all four of them began talking at once, arguing about whose fault it was that I'd been knocked over, until finally the boy with the straight dark hair talked over the rest and told the girl to go and make some coffee.

'Why me?' she protested. 'You all know where the

kettle is. Why do I have to . . .'

'Because you're the best at it,' he interrupted, turning her by the shoulders to face the back of the house. She went, looking back with a grimace at him. She could have been avoiding my eye out of modesty, but then again, to be honest, the most likely explanation was that one glance had told her I wasn't her type.

'Are you one of Casey's friends from school?' the fair-haired one asked, giving me a hand up.

'From the High School? With that hair? And an ear-ing?' the Italian one said.

'She dropped that. At the gate,' I said, gesturing towards the hall table under which the battered packet now lay. All I wanted was to get out as fast as possible. I began to edge towards the door.

'Hey, hold on,' the brother person told me. 'We don't bite, honest. There's nothing to be nervous about. We were just fooling around.'

'Sure,' I said, wrapping my fingers round the door handle.

'Keep trying, Bob. He still looks unconvinced. I'm Colin Jackson,' the fair-haired one said, holding out his hand to me. 'I don't actually live here, I'm happy to say. The human cannonball is Bob Bradley and the one sitting on the stairs with the moronic expression on his face is known to his few remaining friends as Romano Cardosi.'

'I resent that remark,' the Italian one began loudly.

Taking my chance, I pulled the door wide and ran. I took the flight of steps to the path in a couple of bounds and kept going. At last, I leaned hard on the buzzer until my father finally opened the door and let me in.

2

A free lunch

The following day, my father had already gone out by the time I surfaced. There was a note on the kitchen table, some money and a door key.

To be honest, my first reaction was relief. He made me feel uneasy, not to say unwanted. The day before, when we'd been wandering round the museum after a mediocre lunch of soup and wilted salad rolls, he'd been looking past me or glancing over his shoulder all the time, as if hoping somebody more interesting would show up. We had nothing to say to one another and I think he knew it too.

There was some bread left, but nothing to drink except tap water, unless you counted what was left of the gin he'd opened the night before, so I got dressed and went out. It was close to lunchtime anyway. I saw no signs of life at the Bradley house, or, as I now thought of it, the Crazy House. It was just the right size for a private asylum.

It was a kind of overcast day, but dry. I walked towards the city centre, past a park with black metal railings, a short row of modern flats and a couple of expensive-looking hotels, set back from the road in their own leafy grounds. The traffic was relentless.

The only definite thought I had was to see if there was a decent film on somewhere. Further along, the street narrowed and got scruffier. I bought crisps and a can of Coke in a pokey little newspaper shop, but the Sikh who served me said I'd not get a newspaper with what he quaintly called 'the current entertainments' until later in the day. He had as much trouble with my accent as I had with his. I found a wall nearby and leaned against it for a while, watching the people pass.

So this was Glasgow. It looked, sounded and smelled exactly like any other city—grey, noisy and stale. Why was I here? Good question. The short answer was probably my grandmother. (My grandfather, Walter, is still on the scene but he has a nonspeaking role most of the time.)

As soon as I hit my teens, my grandmother, Doris, developed a strange malady unknown to medical science. She became allergic to me. I call it 'late onset emotional asthma'. Or to put it plainly, she discovered she couldn't make my mind up for me any more and she didn't like it.

In term time, when I'm away for most of the day, she forgets this, but in the holidays she remembers. She is always excruciatingly polite, of course — sighs and fading sentences and pink fingernails running up and down the pearls, but I know I'm meant to realize I'm grating on her nerves just by breathing.

I don't take it personally. Apart from her small circle of close friends, *everyone* grates on her nerves. Dear old Walter would too, if he ever opened his mouth.

Nothing throws her off balance. If she was troubled that night by my father's unexpected arrival after so many years, she didn't show it.

She called me downstairs. No warning, no preparation. 'This is Jonathan,' she told him. I was supposed to know who he was without being told.

Well, I did. But he was smaller than I remembered, even when he stood up. He'd lost a lot of hair and behind the glasses there were pouches of skin below his eyes. My first thought was, what are my chances of looking like him when I'm his age?

I was feeling pretty shaken inside, but I got by, answering his questions in monosyllables until the conversation glued itself to a stop. After a few minutes I was dismissed. Audience over.

Later on, once I'd calmed down, I began, astonishingly, to feel a twinge of remorse. He'd looked worn, and defeated, as if he'd been on the receiving end of some hard knocks. As if he'd suffered too. And what did I know about him? Only what Doris had occasionally let fall. He was overseas. He was a busy man. Now I began wondering if maybe he'd wanted to come back and just hadn't managed it. Maybe I was being unfair.

I fell asleep that night without making up my mind either way. The next morning, I was subjected to a pre-dawn kamikaze raid.

'Jonathan, I have something to say.' The blinds were yanked aside. I lay stunned. She was in my room. *My room*. It was like being personally violated.

'We've been discussing this. Jonathan, are you listening to me? Your father has some business in Scotland this summer. We have agreed that it would

15

be an ideal opportunity for you to get to know one an . . .' Her voice faltered. I opened my eyes. She was staring at my posters. The one and only time I have ever seen her at a loss for words. Tragically, it didn't last.

'Please remove those as soon as possible, Jonathan,' she said, making for the door. No reasons. Just do it. 'It's a little late now for breakfast, but I expect you to join us for lunch as usual. How fortunate that Mr Croft didn't require your services at the boatyard this summer.'

I was lost in my thoughts. I didn't notice the guy till he was right in front of me.

'Hello there! You feeling better today?'

It was the Italian-looking one from the day before. Romano. I froze.

'You know, we really felt bad, messing you about like that.'

I was taking in his clothes: white, short-sleeved shirt, small bow-tie, dark trousers, and a dark-green, full-length bibbed apron.

'You like the outfit? Goes with the job. *Eccola!*' His arm gestured dramatically. 'My uncle's place.'

Beside us was a restaurant. Exclusive-looking, totally fronted with one-way dark glass, its name in gold paint above.

'Hey, you want some lunch?'

I hesitated. Out here in the broad light of day, he looked harmless and normal enough . . . Perhaps normal wasn't exactly the right word. With the natural tan and perfect teeth, plus the profile, he was almost too good-looking to be real.

'Come on, the least I can do is get you a free lunch,

after what we did to you yesterday. And if I can tell Casey I've done something good, she might start talking to me again. *Permesso?*' He gestured towards the door.

A free lunch is a free lunch.

Inside, only one of the tables was occupied. Two business types, pushing middle age and paunches, were sitting with a very sleek blonde woman in a dark navy suit, deep in witty conversation and plates of pasta.

There was a quick exchange in Italian between Romano and a stout, balding man, who was polishing wine glasses behind a long counter. He came over, smiled and held out his hand to me.

'Glad to meet you,' he said, in a very strong accent. 'A friend of Mano's is always welcome here. What you like today?'

We agreed on pizza. He pulled out a chair for me at a small table near the swing doors to the kitchen. A middle-aged couple came in from the street, and Romano went to take their order. When he passed me on the way to the kitchen he gave me a big wink. I wasn't sure what, if anything, it was supposed to mean.

It was one very ritzy place. Mirrors and white marble tables, and very soft classical music in the background. I stole a glance at the menu and hoped the burst of Italian had established that I wasn't paying, because the prices were ritzy too.

A girl with black hair tied back in a long pony-tail came in through the front door and went straight past me through the swing doors to the kitchen. A few minutes later, she reappeared wearing a green apron and began a quiet conversation with the older man. She caught my eye and smiled. I smiled back. Not spectacular, but not bad either. She could have done with losing a few pounds and taking off a couple of layers of make-up. She had good legs though.

Romano served the couple first. On his way back he said, '*Ciao*, Diana,' to the girl and smacked her lightly on the rear end. She turned and stuck her tongue out, but it was fairly obvious she liked him. Then he said something in Italian to the old man, who replied briefly. In a couple of moments, he came over with two pizzas, one for himself.

'So tell me, where are you from?' he asked.

'Norfolk. On the coast.'

'So what brings you to Glasgow? What's your name, anyway?'

'Jonathan Moore. I'm on holiday.'

'You're kidding. Is this because you hate sea and sunshine and you love traffic or what? How old are you? You by yourself?'

Unlike the old man's, his accent was pure Glasgow, which was weird considering his looks. He also spoke pretty fast, and I had to concentrate to catch it all.

'I'm sixteen,' I told him. To avoid bringing in my father, I asked, 'Do you live here?'

'You mean here in Glasgow or here?' He gestured at the ceiling above us, then without waiting went on, 'My parents live on the south side, quite far out. Too far for me, so I've got the Bradley's basement. I'm here,' his hand waved again at our surroundings, 'because I need to earn some money if I want to survive another year. Fortunately, my uncle's a sentimental type. Sees life straight through the aorta. He still thinks I'm employable. How's the pizza?'

'It's OK.'

'D'you play cards?'

'Cards? No,' I said, puzzled.

'Well, don't ever play for money, pal. Your face gives everything away. You still don't trust me, do you?'

'Not much.'

He laughed. 'OK. Suppose I expand a little so you can understand yesterday's scenario. We're all students at the Academy. Music and Drama. Colin plays violin, which means he's only mildly eccentric. Bob and I are actors, which means we're more or less certifiable. Yesterday we were just having a few laughs. Just fooling around. I'd have dropped it, but honestly, at first I thought you were a friend of Casey's.'

'Is she Bob's sister?'

He nodded. 'You got any family? Brothers or sisters?'

I shook my head.

'Lucky man,' he observed. 'I have two of each, all younger than me. It's murder, honestly. They're at you the whole time. Steal your shirts, put salt in your beer, you name it.' He shook his head mournfully. 'Casey's not quite that bad, but you have to watch her.'

He began to say something else but paused as the street door opened. Another customer. A stocky, broad-chested man in dark-blue denims and a brown leather jacket. He pulled off his sunglasses and surveyed the room. He looked about thirty.

I heard the older man behind the counter mutter something. To my ignorant ear, it sounded pretty much like swearing. He came round the counter, and Romano rose from the table to face the newcomer.

'We're full up,' the old man said quietly. 'Sorry.'

'You've got plenty empty tables.'

'All booked. Sorry.'

The swing door behind me opened, someone stepped out then retreated. A moment later, it opened again. I glanced sideways. It was a man in a chef's outfit. He was wiping his hands on his apron. Like Romano and his uncle, he was watching the man in the leather jacket very closely. Nobody had raised their voice, but it seemed to me that the atmosphere had changed.

'A'm no' that hungry, as a matter of fact. Just calling by in case Tony was around.'

'He's not here,' the older man said in his heavy accent. 'I don't know where he is. Try Milan. He doesn't come here.'

'But you'd let me know if he did.'

'Sure.'

The man in the leather jacket laughed and nodded his head. He put the sunglasses back on.

'Well, we're still waitin'. Just no' as patient as we were, mebbe. You tell him that, Mario. Tell him that from me, OK? Youse enjoyin' your lunch?' he turned on the slightly startled couple at the table beside him.

'Yes, thank you,' the man said guardedly.

'Glad tae hear it. It's a classy wee place, this. Hard tae beat. You keep in wi' the management, you'll do OK,' he added cryptically. The door swung closed behind him.

Someone pressed a switch somewhere, and the piped music which had stopped some time earlier suddenly flooded the room. Romano went to the door and looked out into the street for a few moments. Then he came back to the table and began to eat.

'Who was that?' I asked.

'Nobody.'

He began telling me what there was to do in the city. It was pretty obvious he wasn't going to explain what had just happened. He asked what my plans were for the rest of the day. I mentioned cinemas. On this subject, the information flowed freely. He knew exactly what was on and where. He was into films, and he talked about directors and camera techniques and so on, using a lot of jargon I didn't understand.

Eventually I pushed my empty plate away. 'Thanks for the meal.'

'You want some ice-cream to finish?'

'No, thanks.'

'So, tell me. Have I restored your confidence in the average Glaswegian or not?'

'I'll tell you, if I ever meet one,' I said.

That struck him as hilarious.

I went on into the city centre and found a cinema he'd told me about, sandwiched between a remnant shop and a second-hand bookstore. The film was a Polish thing, with subtitles, which I found hard to follow, but it was interesting in an off-beat way. Even more interesting was the fact that all the way there and all the way back, I kept noticing sandy-haired men in brown leather jackets.

3

An unsettling evening

My father was back before me. He greeted me curtly, 'You've been out a long time.'

'Why wouldn't I be?'

'You didn't say where you were going.'

'You weren't here when I left,' I said unemotionally.

Stubbing out his cigarette, he announced, 'We ought to get a few things in.' He glanced at his watch. 'You can come if you want to.'

'OK.'

'You don't have to if you don't want to.'

'I'll come. You don't know what I eat.'

'There's not much about you I *do* know.'

So whose fault was that? I shrugged my shoulders.

We drove to the supermarket in silence. It wasn't far away, but the surroundings were totally different, a modern housing estate with an odd, temporary look about it, as if it wasn't sure it wanted to be there at all. A few trees had been planted and vandalized round the edge of the wide car park. The customers were a strange mix too, mostly down at heel, but with a few really well-dressed business types.

'I've made out a list of basics,' he said, handing it to me. His writing was small and precise, like printing. 'See if I've missed anything. Anything you'd particularly like.'

I looked at it for a few seconds then handed it over. 'Looks OK,' I said casually. I grabbed hold of a trolley. We made our way along the aisles. Milk, margarine, cheese, eggs, bacon.

'What did you do this afternoon?' he asked, handing me a multi-pack of baked beans.

'Nothing much.'

'You must have done something.'

'I went to a cinema.'

'Was it good?'

'Not bad.'

'Is that all you can manage? Two-word sentences? Don't you think I'm entitled to a little more than that?'

Two old women, bulging out of sleeveless floral dresses, turned from the tinned peas to look at us. This was better than the TV. He glared back at them.

'Here,' he thrust the list at me. 'You finish it. I need a smoke.' He pulled a wallet from his hip pocket and fished out some notes. 'That should cover it.'

He was waiting just outside the door for me when I finally got it all done. I expected him to make some comment about how long it had taken, but he didn't. Maybe he thought the size of the place had baffled me. But when we were loading up, he said abruptly, 'What's all this for?' He pulled the list out from under a packet of biscuits.

'I'm sorry. I'll take it back.'

'I didn't put soap down.' Then he spotted some more. 'For crying out loud, how much of this stuff is there?' He scanned the scrap of paper in baffled dismay. 'Here. Soup. Ten packets of soup. What are we supposed to do with this?' He gestured angrily at the packs of soap. 'What's the matter with you? Can't you read?'

'No.'

'What?'

'I can't read.'

He flung in the few remaining items and slammed down the boot, narrowly missing my shoulder. 'I've had enough of this,' he said angrily. 'Get in the car.'

'You asked me, I'm telling you.'

'What are you talking about?'

'I can't read,' I said, tight with anger and shame.

'Don't be ridiculous.'

'If you'd bothered to ask any time in the last nine years, you'd have known that much about me!'

His face changed. His whole body stiffened, as if he was hearing something I couldn't. It scared me, because I didn't know what was going to happen, but after a few moments he seemed to come back from wherever he'd been. He lit a fresh cigarette and inhaled slowly. Then he unlocked the driver's door and got in the car. He leaned over and unlocked my side. We were out of the car park and at the first set of traffic lights before he spoke again.

'Let's get this straight. What do you mean, you can't read?'

'I'm dyslexic.'

'What's that supposed to mean?'

'I have a problem with my brain.'

He looked sharply at me. There was an uneasy silence for a few minutes, then he said, 'So how did you get a Maths prize?'

How did he know about that? Had my grandmother told him?

'I'm good at Maths. It's a different thing. Different part of the brain.' Anger was churning my insides. Anger at him for not knowing. For being absent through my entire school career when he should have been around. Anger at myself for losing my cool, for being ashamed of something that wasn't my fault. Oh, I'd exaggerated. I could read. Most words. Most of the time. But not under pressure. Every test, every exam I ever sat, once the clock began ticking, the words before me slipped away like eels on wet ice. I knew I wasn't stupid. Or at least, I hoped I wasn't. What I resented was the way the civilized world forced me to feel stupid most of the time.

'Why didn't your grandmother . . . no, don't bother,' he checked himself. 'Doris wouldn't talk about that sort of thing, would she? What a woman. No fears, no flaws. Take the weak to the wall and shoot them.'

After that he concentrated on the traffic.

Back at the flat he disappeared into his room for a while. I began frying some bacon and eggs. Trying to prove I could do something right, I suppose. For my own satisfaction, though, not his. I wasn't interested in what he thought of me.

When the food was ready, I shouted but he didn't come, so I went through to his room. The door was open. He was kneeling at the window with his hands

25

loose by his sides, his forehead actually touching the glass, staring out, or so it seemed, at the houses opposite. He was so motionless, for a split second I thought he was in some kind of trance, or even dead (which of course he couldn't have been, since he'd have fallen over). Then I saw his Adam's apple move.

He didn't seem to hear me till I raised my voice, and then he just kind of shook his head. Maybe he was into meditation or something. I left him to it, whatever it was.

When at last he came into the kitchen, he sat down in front of the TV, switching over to the seven o'clock news on Channel 4. There was gruesome footage of some car that had plunged off a road a few days before, somewhere near London. The brakes had been tampered with and the driver had died instantly. They were hazarding guesses about the IRA or animal rights activists as usual.

Remembering what he'd said about my grandmother, it crossed my mind that she'd have made a superb terrorist. She was *always* right. Everyone else was wrong unless, of course they agreed with her. But she wouldn't need to shoot anyone or tamper with their car brakes. She'd talk them to death.

I wondered if she'd had a go at him too. His voice had sounded bitter. It occurred to me again that maybe there had been more going on than I knew. He'd been out of my life for nine years, since the accident. I'd assumed he'd wanted it that way. Now I began to wonder just how much she might have had to do with it.

'I kept this warm,' I told him. I had to say it twice.

'They'll never catch them.' He took the plate of

food from me.

'What?'

'Whoever cut that fellow's brakes. This tastes good,' he said through a mouthful. 'They'll never get him. This egg is just the way I like it,' he nodded at me approvingly. 'You see, they've got the technology, but they don't have the intelligence. Do you know the IQ of the average policeman?'

I didn't, but he didn't tell me. He switched over to a sitcom on a different channel. He seemed calmer than before. More relaxed. Maybe whatever he'd been doing had helped. Or did he feel some kind of kinship, both of us against my grandmother?

It was something that had never occurred to me before, but the idea had seeded itself in my brain. Perhaps she was the one who had kept us apart. Put like that, it sounded banal. The official line was that his job had kept him too busy. That was all Doris would ever say. It was always implied that his work (and his pleasures?) were more important to him than his son. Was that what she wanted me to think? I knew as little about him as he did about me.

For instance, I didn't know how his mind worked, what way he would jump. Which was why I'd said nothing about getting mauled at the Crazy House, or getting a free meal, or the man in the restaurant. With someone I knew better, I could have made a good story out of it. How old was he, anyway? There was white in the brown beard, but none in his receding hair.

I didn't even know what his job was. Was he here in Glasgow to do business for his firm or what? Or had he lost his job and come north to look up boyhood pals in the hope of finding something else? He was knocking back the gin a bit, but it didn't seem to affect him much. On the other hand there was a strange edginess in his manner, a kind of haunted look in his eyes, as if something was closing in on him, like maybe a sense of failure.

I speared my last piece of cold fried egg, irritated by all these questions, not even sure I wanted to know the answers. I had enough problems of my own without crippling myself worrying about his.

4

A quick trip . . .

That night I woke up out of a wild dream where I was being attacked by a couple of dentists. Except they were only pretending to be dentists. They had all the shiny equipment, and the spotless white uniforms, but I fought back when they told me I needed all my teeth out. I have good teeth; all my problems are deeper inside my head.

The bedroom was airless, so I hauled myself out of bed and wedged the window open. A few minutes after I'd crawled back under the sheet, there was a faint thud. It sounded as if the wad of old magazines I'd folded under the frame had slipped. I hauled myself back out of bed again, to find it still in place.

The street below was dim. No movement, not even a cat in search of mouse meat. I checked my watch. Nearly half past two. The street lights would be burning for another couple of hours. I couldn't see the stars. Back home on a summer night like this there would be darkness, and a couple of owls screeching at one another, or a dog fox slinking along the hedgerow, and stars all over the place.

Then as I watched, a car door opened on the far side of the street. A dark Ford Sierra. Dark blue? In the orange light of the street lamps, I couldn't tell. Nor could I judge the colour of the leather jacket on the man who was crossing from my side of the road towards the car. But I'd have gone to the gallows swearing it was the same man, the one who'd come into the restaurant looking for Tony, the man Romano said was 'Nobody'.

Very carefully, I let the curtain fall back into place till there was only a thin strip of space left to look through. The man was leaning on the open door of the car, as if talking to someone inside. He straightened, looked up and down the street, and over at my side. Then he got into the car. Nothing happened for maybe three or four minutes. Then it pulled out, and, without lights, went slowly down towards the main road.

I stood watching for a while, the musty curtain making my nose itch. Nothing happened, except my bare stomach got chilled from the open window.

Next morning was a re-run of the day before. I didn't wake till nearly eleven and didn't even hear my father leave. I showered, dressed and made myself a cheese sandwich. The kitchen stank of cigarette butts, which I covered with a plate. He could clean up his own debris.

I couldn't get what I'd seen out of my head. It was interesting. I knew Glasgow was supposed to be famous for its gangs, like in that film, *Comfort and Joy*, where they smash up all the ice-cream vans. It was a good story. Then I told myself to forget the fantasy. Real life is never that interesting. If it was, they'd never need to make films. Or fool about pretending to be in one, as the Bradley boy and his friends had.

I wondered if the one called Romano would tell Casey he'd met me. I wondered where she was. I was staring at their door, trying to imagine what she might be doing, when it opened and the brother came out. He stood looking at the day for a couple of seconds then started to go down the steps. Suddenly his arms flew up into the air and he catapulted forward, head first. From our window, I could only see their gate and the top of the steps, because of the bushes. When he didn't reappear, it occurred to me that all was not well . . .

When I got there, he was sitting up, holding both hands to his face, moaning. There was a terrific amount of blood all over the place.

'Hey, what happened?' I said, breathless from my one minute dash over to him. 'You OK?'

He just moaned some more. I stumbled up the steps and pushed my thumb practically through the doorbell. I tried the door. It opened. Flinging it wide, I yelled for help. I was in a sweat. I didn't know whether to go back to him, or what. There was a phone on the hall table. My shaking fingers were clumsy on the buttons when the girl appeared at the top of the inside stairs.

'What're you doing here? Was that you ringing the . . .'

'Your brother . . . He fell . . .' I began, then a man's voice in my ear was asking which service I wanted. 'Ambulance,' I told him hurriedly. The girl darted

31

past me, wailing, 'Bob! Bob!' Then the whole thing became farcical for a few moments, because I couldn't remember the name of the street, or the number, so I had to get the new voice on the line to hold on, while I shouted at the girl for information.

Somehow the pair of us got him inside, and on to a kind of low armchair inside their front room. He was a bit more coherent. He wouldn't lie down, insisting he'd choke. She ran out and was back in a couple of seconds with a pair of pale cream towels. He took one and started telling her he was fine.

'Don't be an idiot,' she said wildly, 'you're not fine at all. You're bleeding all over the place. What happened?'

'I doan know,' he mumbled. 'I thing I broke by dose.'

I stood there with my hands in my pockets, feeling useless. There wasn't anything I could do, but I didn't want to leave.

'Thangs for helbig,' he said in my direction. The girl looked round. I think she'd forgotten I was there.

I said the first thing that came into my head. 'You've messed your sweatshirt.'

She looked down at herself. 'It doesn't matter.'

'You bedder go and pud it in somb water,' her brother told her.

'Bob, would you stop trying to organize me? There's an ambulance coming. It's you we're worrying about, not me.'

'Who called a abulance?'

'Me,' I said.

'I subbose I need one. It's not really sore. I thing the bleeding's stobbed.' He lifted the towel away then pressed it back. 'Maybe dot,' he admitted.

'Make sure he stays put,' she told me. 'I'd better get the keys. What else do I need?'

'Um. Money?' I suggested. 'You might have to hang around.'

'OK,' she said, biting her lip.

The ambulance was there before she reappeared. I shouted up the stairwell to wherever she was, then went to open the front door.

'He's in the front room,' I told the ambulance man, a short, grey-haired man in a one-piece green overall. I stood on the doorstep and took a couple of deep breaths, seeing Bob fall again. There were long skid marks on the gravel where he'd landed. I looked at the path more closely.

When I came back into the sitting room, the man, now wearing disposable gloves, and with a plastic apron on top of his overall, was taking off our towel very gently and putting a clean white wad over Bob's nose, taping it down with a practised hand.

'Right then, son, think you can make it out to the van? Hold on, you want to go round his other side,' he told me, when the taping was finished.

The girl followed behind. Once her brother was safely inside, I stood back.

'You coming?' the man asked.

'Um, I don't know,' I began.

'Please. You're the only one who saw what happened,' the girl said hurriedly. She was already inside.

'You sure?'

'Make up your mind, lad. I'm closing this door,' the man warned me. I stepped up into the van.

5

. . .to the hospital

Nobody said much during the short drive to the hospital. The girl sat holding her brother's hand. I sat wishing I had the nerve to hold her other one.

Once there, Bob had to sit in a wheelchair. He protested. The ambulance man insisted. We followed them through automatic doors into the Casualty waiting area.

I stood around while the girl gave details. A broad-chested nurse in a blue dress wouldn't let her follow when Bob was wheeled away. We found seats and prepared to wait.

The room was about forty feet square. Off-white walls, grey moulded-plastic seats, pale grey floor. Two cheap and forgettable views of hillsides on either side of the cold drinks machine against the far wall. The usual worn magazines in a heap on two low tables at the side. Half a dozen other people besides us.

'At least they're seeing him quickly,' I said.
'I suppose so.'

'He'll be OK.'

She was leaning forward with her hands clasped between her knees. Her shiny dark-brown hair fell forward like a curtain, hiding her face.

Across from us, a child of seven or so with unkempt hair and a home-made bandage round her knee was leaning against her mother, who was ignoring a whining toddler. A glum-faced man beside me looked as if he'd been here for weeks. Or months.

'I keep wondering who I could speak to.' She straightened up.

'What d'you mean?'

'Well, my Dad's in Malawi just now, but this is where he works. And there's probably somebody on call who could . . .' She broke off as the outside doors swished open and two men in grubby overalls came in. One had a hand wrapped in an oily, bloodstained rag. The other went to the desk, and spoke to the clerk. After only a few minutes a youngish Asian-looking doctor came in and took the injured man away down the corridor.

'I don't see how it could have happpened,' she said glumly. 'Was he running? Did you see him?'

'I don't know,' I said awkwardly. I picked at my fingernails for a few seconds. 'It wasn't your . . .'

'What?'

'Nothing.'

'Hey, this is silly, isn't it?' she made a face. 'I don't know your name. I'm Hope Bradley.'

'Jon Moore. That boy Colin called you Casey.'

'It started up as a family joke. When I was small I always made a mess at mealtimes. When I was in my high chair. So my mother said I wasn't a Hope, I was a hopeless case. She must have said it more than once, and Bob was about six, and he started calling me Casey. Hope is a terrible name, anyway. I wouldn't wish it on my worst enemy.' She brushed away a strand of hair that had fallen across her face. 'What were you going to say, before?'

'Anne-Marie McCafferty?' the big nurse in the blue dress called out. The mother with the two children pulled herself up, gathered the children and followed.

'Just that we did the right thing,' I improvised, when Casey waited for me to answer.

'Well, you did. I think I'd have panicked, on my own.'

'You got the towels.'

'I suppose so.' She shivered, though the room wasn't cold. 'I just hate sitting here. I can't see why they won't let us go in with him. Well, I can, but they might at least tell us what's happening. I feel I should be doing something, but I don't know what. I just wish Dad was here.'

'They're never here when you need them.'

'Aren't they?'

'Maybe you've been lucky so far.'

'Haven't you?'

'Not spectacularly.'

'That's tough,' she said seriously.

'Don't worry about it. I'm surviving.'

We sat without talking for a while after that. There was a regular stream of people coming and going. Porters, nurses in uniforms that somehow always looked a size too tight, injured members of the public with haggard relatives. At one point there was a diversion, in the shape of a ramshackle old drunk in a long dark raincoat, who made his way unsteadily over to the desk, then was told to sit down. He began mumbling to himself. We all glanced at him and away. After a few minutes, a porter came in, got him up on his feet and escorted him firmly out of the door.

'Comes in every week,' the porter confided to the entire waiting room. 'Nothing wrong with him. He's after a clean bed and a free meal. Nice work if you can get it, eh?'

'D'you think it's right to give them money?' Casey said quietly.

'Who?' I asked.

'People like that. Down and outs. I sometimes do, but you wonder if they just spend it on drink. So you're not really helping, are you?'

'They're past being helped, once they get to that stage.'

'Nobody's past being helped. Don't be so cynical.'

'You can't help someone who doesn't want to be helped.'

'I suppose . . . Would you say you'd had a sheltered childhood?'

The question took me by surprise, but she was waiting for an answer, so I had to think about it. I thought about it. Wrecked, wretched, stifled maybe. Sheltered, no.

'I don't think so,' I told her. I was thinking how weird this was. She hardly knew me, but here we were, side by side, talking as if we were old buddies. I supposed it was because she was in some kind of mild shock, and I just happened to be there. I can't say I minded. The chairs were jammed up close, and I could smell her perfume, or it could have been shampoo. It smelled like apples.

'I think I have,' she went on. 'In some ways. My parents are still very much together which isn't all that normal these days. And surgeons are well paid, so Mum never worked after Bob was born. She does a lot of charity work, and things in the church, but she's always been there. I suppose I should be rebelling or something.'

'How old are you?'

'Fifteen. Sixteen in November.'

'There's still time.'

'No, it's too late. I'll never be a rebel. I get mad at them sometimes, but basically I like them too much. It's a problem. I think I'm failing my generation. You look like a rebel.'

'It's camouflage. I'm incredibly middle-aged and conservative underneath.'

'I believe you. Of course, I'm very naive for my age.'

'Do you like your brother too?'

'Old bossy Bob?' she grinned. 'As brothers go, he's OK, even if sometimes I feel like bouncing his head off the nearest brick wall. Eeugh. Sick joke, right?' she grimaced.

Again we sat without talking for a few minutes. 'Your friend Romano . . .' I began, then hesitated.

'How do you know . . . oh yes, you met them all, didn't you?' Her voice changed. 'What about him?'

'He um . . . He said you . . . Well, we were talking about how he and your brother were fooling about . . .'

'When were you talking to Mano?'

Ignoring the question, I went on, 'And he said

38

you . . . um . . . liked playing practical jokes.'

When the words were out, I wished them back. But I had to know.

'Did he say that? About me?'

'Uhuh.'

'Talk about the pot and the kettle,' she said cryptically. 'Not that I'm bothered what he thinks. Mano Cardosi is the original complete male chauvinist.'

The withering way she said it, it sounded like a life sentence. No appeal and throw away the key. I probed a little deeper, feeling like a criminal myself.

'So you wouldn't play a trick on him?'

She looked at me curiously.

'Why?'

'I just wondered.'

'You're making me feel uneasy. Did you have something planned?'

'Me? No.'

'You have.'

'No. It's not my kind of thing.'

She had to leave it at that, because the woman in the blue uniform interrupted, calling out, 'Is there someone here for Robert Bradley?'

I didn't go with her, though she asked if I wanted to. I needed a chance to think.

It sounded as if she was telling the truth, that she hadn't planned a practical joke on them. OK, so I didn't know her very well. But on the other hand my instincts told me that a girl with eyes like hers ought to be trusted. The mouth and the eyebrows also seemed essentially sincere . . .

So was I to trust my instincts and her eyebrows?

Just because a girl smelled good, it didn't mean she was telling the truth. But if she was, what was the explanation for the length of fine wire I was fingering in my pocket, which I had found on their path tied to the railings and which, judging by the mark on the stem of a rose bush opposite, had just done a neat job of tripping up Bob Bradley?

6

A few home truths

Casey came back to me in the waiting room after about twenty minutes, looking miserable. With her was a grey-haired female in a white coat who eyed me through dark-rimmed spectacles as if I was something suspicious she'd spotted under a microscope.

'I understand you saw the accident,' she said briskly.

'Sort of,' I replied.

'You did or you didn't?'

'I saw him take off. I didn't see him land.'

'Why not?'

'There was a bush in the way.'

'Well, that's not much help, is it?'

She made it sound as if it was all my fault. I stared at her name badge. Doctor Macsomething. She turned to Casey.

'I'm sorry, Hope,' her tone warmed noticeably, 'I'm afraid we will have to keep him in. It's better just to make sure. Telephone in the morning. Are you going to be all right?'

'Oh, I'm fine. Isn't there visiting at night?'

'Certainly. I think it's seven till eight, but don't worry if that doesn't suit.'

'What's wrong?' I asked.

'He can't remember what happened,' Casey said. The doctor was already walking away. 'They want to keep him in overnight.'

'She's a real charmer, that one. What's wrong with him?'

'His nose is broken. He's got stitches as well. They want to keep an eye on him because we don't know if he hit his head. And because Dad's the boss, more than anything else. Nobody wants to take the responsibility of letting him go until the consultant sees him. If Bob remembers, he'll get out tomorrow.'

'What d'you mean, the boss?'

'He's the Professor of Surgery here,' she said, almost apologetically.

I digested that new bit of information then said, 'So what are you going to do?'

'I don't know. Go home and wait, I suppose.'

'Pity they went to Malawi,' I said, as we stepped out into the sunshine, 'but I suppose they've done Blackpool by now.'

'They're not on holiday. My uncle works at a mission hospital there. Dad's relieving him for three weeks. We can go this way.' She turned into what looked like a dead end. 'There's a short cut through the car park.' She stopped suddenly. 'Do you... should you phone your parents?'

'What?'

'I mean, we didn't check with them. D'you want to let your parents know where you are? Everything happened so fast, I didn't...' She broke off, stood where she was, and closed her eyes. 'Oh, this is so stupid...' she said, desperately wiping her hand over them. But I'd seen the tears.

I stood there for a moment or two, feeling awkward and inadequate, aware that the people passing were looking at us with interest.

'He'll be fine,' I said, wishing I could think of something less pathetic to say.

'Blood sugar.'

'What?' I said, startled.

'My blood sugar's low. That's what's wrong with me. I need to eat,' she said firmly. She'd dug a piece of crumpled pink tissue out of her shoulder bag and was wiping desperately at her face. 'Are you hungry?'

'I didn't have any breakfast,' I lied.

We ended up in a McDonald's. Right on the doorstep, it dawned on me that I didn't have any money.

'What's wrong?'

'I've no cash,' I said.

'You can pay me back.'

We ordered burgers and rolls and wedged ourselves into a table away from the plate-glass windows and the busy street.

She asked where I came from. 'You won't have heard of it,' I said, but to my surprise she had. It turned out that she'd been born in Norwich and lived there the first six years of her life. She couldn't remember being in my village, but she remembered seaside holidays at Sheringham along the coast. I said the lifeboat station was still there, and the putting green up on the cliff. Neither of us could place the house they'd rented.

What else did we talk about? I honestly can't remember. I was trying very hard to sound witty and clever. I made her laugh a couple of times. She had a nice laugh, not a titter like some girls. We talked about school, about music we liked and loathed. I talked a lot of rubbish, but she didn't seem to mind. Sitting there with her, I felt as if nothing else mattered. There must have been other people round about us, but I was deaf and blind to them. I sucked the smallest possible drops of Coke up my straw and hoped the hamburger would last for ever.

Nothing does. Two female voices shattered the idyll.

'Hi, Casey!' they chorused.

She introduced me as a friend of Bob's, which was interesting. There was a lot of giggling from the other two and exclusive, slightly phoney chat about what they'd been doing and mutual friends from school.

After a few minutes, I excused myself. I hung about in the toilet for quite a while. I think I washed my hands three times.

The partition walls were so flimsy that when a conversation began through on the female side, it was impossible not to hear it once the hot-air dryer switched itself off.

'She's not giving much away though.'

'Like his telephone number?'

'Get lost.'

'I saw you, Eleanor. Flutter, flutter, flutter, with the eyelashes. You practically blew us all away.'

'He is *not* my type. I wouldn't have thought he was Casey's either. Little Miss Prim. Wait till I tell Christine.'

'He's not bad looking. The hair's awful, but he's got nice broad shoulders.'

'Just like the motorway.'

There were snorts of laughter.

'Maybe he's got hidden depths.'

The snorts increased. Then there was a muffled thud as if their door had opened. I heard a child's high voice, and a mother's sharp one.

I washed my hands for the fourth time, splashing cold water on my face. Somebody had dropped a ballpoint on the floor. I used it to inscribe my opinion of Eleanor on the wall beside the wash-basins.

When I went back into the restaurant, my heart sank even further. No sign of Casey. Our table had been cleared. I stood around for a few moments like a knotless thread and then made for the door.

She was standing a few feet away. She turned and gave me a wide smile.

'I thought you'd gone,' I said.

'The waitress was getting agitated.'

'So what's next?'

'Home, I suppose.'

I looked up and down the sun-filled street. Scores of people, old, young, white, brown, shabby and well-dressed. Couples arm in arm. An Indian woman in a shimmering blue and silver sari with a dancing toddler in bright pink shorts and T-shirt. Cars roaring past. A florist's van with boxes of cut carnations being unloaded.

'I don't know where we are,' I said.

'That is so sad.'

'I'm breaking your heart.'

'And you owe me money.'

'If you don't show me the way home, you'll never get it back.'

'Oh well, in that case . . .'

She didn't know me well enough to realize that part of my relief in finding her still there was because I have a lousy sense of direction. Normally when I go anywhere, I try to memorize landmarks. Walking with her, I hadn't bothered. Besides that, the different accents here unsettled me. Scottish people all seemed to talk so fast. It sounds stupid, but I actually felt like a foreigner. And the buildings were different too. Rising two storeys above the ground-floor shops, they were mostly soot-blackened sandstone, not red brick or flint and brownstone like at home.

After we'd walked about a half mile, we turned a corner and crossed at some traffic lights. Then I began recognizing some buildings I'd passed the day before, like the hotel with the big row of willow trees.

At our gate, I asked her to wait so I could run up and get my wallet. But I couldn't. Nothing happened when I pressed on the bell for our flat. I'd left so fast, I hadn't thought of the key.

'The old man's still out,' I told her. 'I can't pay you back.'

'Never mind. Come over tomorrow, once Bob gets home.' She added with a sudden sigh, 'I hope.'

'Hey, don't start that again.'

She made a face and flicked at the strap and buckle of her bag. 'Thanks for helping,' she said finally.

It sounded like goodbye. I groped for more conversation.

'Thanks for the lunch. That's the second free one I've had in two days. Your friend Romano gave me a pizza yesterday. Did he tell you?'

'I haven't seen him. I wonder if I ought to phone him,' she added as a quick afterthought. 'He'd want to know, wouldn't he?'

'I suppose he would. What about the other one, the one with the fair hair?'

'Colin's got some kind of gardening job somewhere. And his parents won't be in. We could phone Mano at the restaurant.'

Since she'd said 'we' and she didn't actually say goodbye after that, I followed her up the path and into her house. For one thing, I didn't have anywhere else to go.

I was also thinking that it might be interesting to have a couple of words with Romano—on the subject of thin wire and rose bushes. And there was something else. I wondered if he'd be interested to know that the man in the brown leather jacket had been watching the Bradley's house in the middle of the night.

7

Phoning Romano

We went upstairs to a small book-lined room on the
half-landing. While Casey knelt on the floor with the
telephone directory, I had a good look round.

Two tall, locked filing cabinets. On the pine desk, a
gilt framed photograph of a dark-haired woman. I
guessed it must be her mother. Another showed all
four of them, the father and Bob in kilts and dark
jackets with fancy silver buttons. The Professor had
gold-rimmed glasses, not much hair and a grin like a
Cheshire cat, as if the photographer had said something hilarious. I felt as if I'd seen him before, and
said so to Casey.

'He was on television, maybe you saw it. They
made it a while ago, but it was just broadcast last
month. His department's doing a new surgical technique. He didn't like it much because his bald bits
were so obvious. He still thinks he's got hair.'

The wall behind the desk was all pin-board,
covered with typed papers, notes, circulars and lists.
There was a poster of two dolphins arcing across a

white-crested wave. Underneath, it said, 'Our help is from the Lord who made heaven and earth.' I didn't get the connection.

Casey found the number at last. When she got through, she asked for Romano, without giving her name.

'Well, yes,' she told the person at the other end. 'I'm phoning for Robert Bradley.' Another pause. 'I suppose so.' A few more seconds, then she recited her own phone number. 'Thanks very much,' she said and hung up.

'Why didn't you say who you were?'

'She'd think I was one of his doting females.'

'How many does he have?'

'About a hundred, I should imagine, and I'm not one of them.'

All of a sudden, I felt absurdly happy.

'So what's happening?'

'They're too busy. She said she'd get him to phone as soon as there's a lull.' She took the phone book from me and slotted it back on the shelf. 'I'm still hungry. Are you?'

So I found myself down in their kitchen. It was all white and grey. White units, grey worktops, white curtains with grey stripes. There were some less immaculate details, like the grubby red wellington boots in one corner, the slightly burnt oven gloves beside the cooker, the pin-board with postcards, photographs, money-off vouchers, and so on. Plus a strange collection of battered pottery cows on the window ledge at the sink.

'Like them?' Casey asked.

'They're different.'

'Mum went to a pottery class for ten weeks. She got totally addicted to Highland cattle. If I heat a tin of spaghetti, would you eat half?'

'Sure.'

'Does your mother take up hobbies all the time?'

'She's dead.'

The tin-opener dropped from Casey's fingers and shot across the floor.

'It's a long time ago,' I said. I got up and retrieved the tin-opener. 'Nearly nine years.'

She looked away, spooning the spaghetti slowly out of its tin and into a pot. 'Well...' She bit her lip. 'Trust me... I... I'm sorry... I wouldn't have...' Her voice trailed away awkwardly. 'How did she... It's none of my...'

'It was a freak accident. A wheel broke off a container lorry, bounced along the road and smashed into them.'

Casey didn't say anything. I talked to the pottery cow in my hand. 'They operated at the hospital, but she never regained consciousness. Russell got thrown out of the buggy. She'd pushed it away.'

'Is that your brother? Was he all right?'

I couldn't answer her. I was back in the room where I'd seen him for the last time, two years after the accident. Up till then, they'd kept me from him, barricaded me round with reasonable excuses: it was too far, I would be in the nurses' way, I could come the next time... Adult excuses which my eight-year-old, nine-year-old mind accepted without question.

I saw him exactly as he'd been, lying in a pathetic tangle of sheets and gaudy knitted cover, grey eyes watching us, mouth moving soundlessly, fingers scrabbling at the pillowcase. And me standing there like a fool with a football for him, because it was his fifth birthday. Knowing only then that he'd never use it, that he probably didn't even know what it was.

The visit changed nothing for Russell, but everything for me. On the long drive back home, I'd begun to look objectively at my grandmother and to dislike what I saw. I'd stared at the immaculate greying curls on the back of her head, with only one thought in mine. Why had she let me buy a football for someone who couldn't even sit up by himself? The answer was obvious. She didn't care. Didn't care what the present was, didn't care how I felt, didn't care whether Russell could feel or not.

The smells of that sad, terrible echoing room had stayed with me for days ... Chrysanthemums. Eye-watering pine disinfectant. Floor polish. I'd never gone back. Not long afterwards, my grandfather, vocal for once, communicated the fact that Russell had died of influenza. I'd felt guilty and overwhelmingly relieved.

'How old were you?'

Casey's voice broke into my remembering.

'Seven. Nearly eight.'

'Do you ... think about her a lot?'

Easier if I didn't. Too much to remember but not enough. Not enough to remember what her voice had been like. She'd sung me to sleep every night and I could still remember some of the songs, but not how her voice had sounded. Funny how that bothered me more than not remembering her face.

'What about your brother?'

I told her briefly about Russell. She put two plates

of spaghetti on the table. Buttered toast on another plate. She brought a carton of orange juice out of the fridge, glasses from a wall cabinet.

'Your father must have been shattered,' she said.

'He might have been, for all I know.'

She looked at me, bewildered.

'He took off after the accident. Went abroad somewhere. I was left with my grandparents. Last week he zoomed back, without warning. This is supposed to be the holiday when we get to know one another again.'

'And are you?'

There was a terrible directness in her questions. Later I decided it was because she was so open in everything. What Casey said was what she meant. She never lied to people and she expected them to be honest back. But that day, I couldn't handle it.

I put the cow carefully down on the table and picked up my fork. 'You realize I've just told you more of my fascinating family history than I've ever told most of my pals? I mean, guys I've known for years?' I said, jokily.

'I won't tell anyone, if that's what's worrying you.'

'Not even big brother?'

'Not if you don't want me to.'

'How have you survived this long?'

'Sorry?'

I tried to find words to say what I meant.

'Well, you're . . . Like, here you are, alone in the house with a boy you hardly know. What would your mother say?' I found myself thinking of the bitchy females in the toilets. I knew already what they'd thought.

'She'd probably say, "Was spaghetti and toast the

best you could manage, dear? That's hardly enough for a growing boy." '

'Your friends didn't seem to warm to me.'

'They're not really friends, I just know them from school. I used to hang around with them a lot last year but they . . .'

The phone shrilled loudly from the hallway. I followed her through. It was Romano. She told him what had happened, including my part in the business, then there was a longish pause. She put her hand over the receiver. 'He's trying to see if he can get away,' she told me.

'Can I speak to him,' I asked, 'once you've finished?'

'What for?'

'Just about the meal he bought me,' I improvised.

The phone came to life again, and I saw her face fall slightly. 'OK,' she said. 'I didn't know what else to do.' Noises from the other end. 'No, it's all right. I'll manage. I'll get a bus.' There was some more from his end, then she said, 'He wants to speak to you.' She handed the phone over.

'Hi,' I said.

'How is she?' was Romano's first question. 'Is she OK?'

'I think so. It's difficult to say.'

'Because she's standing beside the phone?'

'You could put it that way.'

'Tell her to go and do something.'

'Like what?'

'I don't know. Pack pyjamas for him. Personal stereo. Think of something.'

I turned to Casey. 'He's asking if you've got

53

pyjamas looked out for Bob.'

'I'll go and see what's clean,' she said, beginning to leap up the stairs. 'Tell him it's seven till eight, visiting. I don't know which ward,' she shouted as she disappeared.

'She's gone,' I told Romano.

'So how is she? We're doing a blasted wedding this afternoon, and we're short as it is, but if she's hysterical...'

'No, she's OK, I think.'

'So what happened?'

'Somebody strung a wire across the steps.'

'What!'

I said it again, describing more fully what I'd seen. There was a brief burst of what sounded like earthy Italian. He began to speak, but I interrupted, watching the top of the stairs all the time, not knowing how long I had before Casey reappeared.

'That man who came in to the restaurant yesterday...'

'What about him?'

'He was prowling around here last night. This morning,' I corrected myself, 'about three o'clock.'

I had to explain how I had seen him. There was a silence when I finished. Not silence exactly, because there was a machine rumbling quietly in the background somwhere, but no voice.

Then he said abruptly, 'Listen to me. Don't ask questions. I want you to go down into my flat. Go to the bedroom...'

'Me? What are you...'

'Shut up and listen! Don't tell Casey. Make up some kind of story. You'll think of something.

54

There's a blue sports bag in the bottom of the wardrobe. Are you listening?'

'Sure, but what if she...'

'Bring it here, to the restaurant. And don't bother trying to open it. I don't have a key anyway.' There was another quick Italian phrase. 'Look, I have to go. You sure you can find this place?'

'I think so,' I said hesitantly.

'Pal, you better know so. Or we're both in trouble. Casey too. So you better get on with it. But do it yourself. Don't get her into this. See you later.'

'What was all that about?' Casey's voice fell like a blow on my ears, and I jumped like a guilty man.

8

The bag in the basement

She had a pile of stuff in her arms—red pyjamas, a toilet bag, a folded brown towel. Without realizing, I'd turned to face the front door, so I hadn't a clue how long she'd been standing there. Desperately I tried to think what hearing one side of the conversation would have told her.

'Well?'

'Well what?'

'He thinks I'm not coping, doesn't he?'

'I don't know. Are you?'

'Don't you start.' She dropped her bundle on the carpet and pulled open the door of a small cupboard beneath the stairs. After rummaging inside for a few moments she emerged with a small beige rucksack, into which she began stuffing the pyjamas.

'He um . . . He wants me to get something from the flat.'

Her brows came together in surprise.

'You?'

'Yes?'

'Why?'

We were beginning to sound like a loser's game of Scrabble.

'Something he needs.'

'For Bob?'

'He didn't say. I've just to pick it up and take it along to the restaurant. I don't think it's anything important, but I said I was going to be passing...' I faltered.

'Is something wrong?'

'No, it's not important.' I didn't know what to do with my hands. I folded my arms, just to stop them dangling. The whole thing was getting beyond me. I didn't know how long I could improvise like this, with her big brown eyes on me. What was I getting involved in? Good grief, what was I already involved in?

'How do I get down there?'

'I'll show you,' she said slowly. 'You look funny. Are you all right?'

'Indigestion,' I said, pressing my stomach. 'I drank the Coke too fast.'

I suspected she didn't believe me, but she let it pass.

She pulled open a door beside us, which I'd supposed was another cupboard. She switched on a light, showing a curving flight of steep uncarpeted steps. I started down them. She came right behind me. I stopped, turned and she landed up against me, which under any other circumstances would have been fantastic. We untangled ourselves.

'Look, Casey. I think I can manage.'

'No, I think I'll come too.'

Keep her out of it, Romano had warned me. My mind raced through all the possible reasons I could give for wanting to go down by myself. Each was flimsier than the one before. I gave up.

The stairs opened into a dim living room. High in the wall opposite were two long horizontal windows with half-closed venetian blinds. I glimpsed the shapes of bushes and shrubs and a strip of blue sky outside.

Apart from a couple of bright yellow canvas deck chairs, all the furniture was old. There was a pricey-looking music centre and a stack of CDs in one corner. He had a lot of unframed posters on the walls, mostly black and white. Humphrey Bogart, James Dean, others I didn't recognize.

I made for what I assumed was the bedroom, with Casey hot on my heels. Once again I did my expert skid to a halt routine. This time she anticipated it and stopped short.

'Look, it's something in his bedroom. Boys only,' I said, improvising desperately.

Her face went pink. 'Oh. All right,' she said, looking embarrassed. 'I'll wait here.'

I closed the bedroom door. The wardrobe was a huge mahogany thing with mirrored doors. It was so big the house had probably been built round it. I grimaced angrily at my face in the mirror. There was a sudden burst of music from the living room, then voices, then different music. It sounded as if she was trying every radio channel on the dial.

There was nothing on the floor of the wardrobe except piles of magazines and two pairs of worn, slightly smelly Reeboks. Then I realized he must have meant the narrow drawer at the bottom.

The bag was there, zipped and locked. Nothing rattled inside when I shook it. It was well filled, but I couldn't tell anything from the shape. Well, it was none of my business.

Closing the drawer, I went back into the living room. Casey had switched off the radio and was peering up at the window. I began to say something.

'Shh,' she gestured at me urgently. 'Listen,' she whispered. 'There's somebody in our back garden.'

She had closed the blinds until they were only open a crack. I couldn't see anything moving.

'Maybe it was a cat . . .' I began.

'Shh! He just went past the window. He'll have to come back. You can't get through the rhododendrons that side.' All this in a whisper.

I thought she was probably imagining it, but I hoisted myself up on the table that stood against the wall and peered out, not touching the blinds. If I hadn't had one hand resting on the wall, I think I'd have fallen backwards, because a shadow fell right in front of me. I held my breath.

Another shadow—a pair of trouser-clad legs. A man's voice spoke, just a couple of words. From somewhere to our left, above our heads, there was a kind of creaking noise then what sounded like feet scuffling against the stonework.

'What is it?' Casey asked.

My turn to say 'Shh.' I listened, every nerve straining. My mouth had suddenly gone dry.

'There's someone upstairs,' she said quite indignantly, after a couple of moments. 'They must have come in through the pantry window.'

'How do we get out of here?' I asked urgently. 'Where's the door?'

She caught my meaning at last and scurried on tiptoe through a door on our left. A short flight of stone stairs led up to a green-painted wooden door. She pulled at the handle. 'Here, let me,' I said, pushing past her.

'No, it's locked. It's a double throw. We'll never do it.'

We went back into the main room.

'OK. We telephone,' I said hurriedly.

'Who?'

'The police, who d'you think?' I said roughly. I'd seen a phone in the bedroom. But before I could get to it, there were sounds on the internal stairs.

'Quick! Here!' Casey caught at what I thought was a light switch and pulled open a narrow panel in the wall. I fell in behind her. She drew the door shut and we were in total darkness. The bag slithered from my hands, landing with a soft thud somewhere at my feet, but I couldn't bend to get it. Our backs were up against shelves of some kind and the door was pressing on us. There was no room to move. I could feel her shaking.

We heard the room door open and close. A low voice said, 'You take this room.'

Then there were quiet sounds. Like drawers being pulled out and closed, lids lifted and gently dropped. My heart was thumping louder than any noise they were making. I shut my eyes. The noises came closer. Casey's fingers tightened on mine.

9

Breaking point

They say your whole life rushes in front of you when you're facing disaster. Maybe it doesn't work unless you've lived longer. All I thought about was trying to breathe without sneezing, because the dust in that cupboard was awful. So I was trying to breathe out all the time without breathing in, and my neck and jaw muscles were rigid.

After what felt like hours but was maybe fifteen minutes, I couldn't stand it any longer. There were no sounds at all from the room, and I was sure that if I didn't get into the open I was going to pass out. More in desperation than courage, I pushed the panel and stepped into the room. I looked round, saw nobody and collapsed against the wall.

'Is it OK?' came Casey's whisper.

'Could be,' I said, trying to rub my arms back to life. Then the sneeze finally came. I waited for somebody to leap out from one of the other rooms. Nothing happened.

Casey came out cautiously and began brushing

dust off her jeans and the sleeves of her sweatshirt.

'You should get Romano to clean in there some time,' I said in a low voice, gesturing to the cupboard behind us. With the panel in place it was invisible, part of the wallpaper again.

'We don't use it,' she whispered back. 'I think it was bigger, before the toilet was put in on the other side. The people before us kept their home-made wine in it. Come on, we'd better phone the police now.'

'I don't know. They might still be upstairs. They'd hear us lift a phone.'

'But we can't let them get away. They might be doing anything up there.' She stared at me in mingled frustration and anger. 'Well, I'm going to. I don't care...'

'Casey, wait,' I caught hold of her arm.

'Let go! What do you think you're...'

'Keep your voice down,' I said urgently. 'Just wait a minute, will you?'

'This is my house and there are burglars in it,' she whispered fiercely, pulling her arm free.

'I don't think they're ordinary burglars...' I began.

'So what are they? Tourists?' she said scathingly.

I didn't know what to do, I just felt that I didn't want the police on the scene. Because I was getting more certain by the minute that the blue holdall between my feet was what the intruders had been looking for. Ordinary burglars would have taken the stereo, for one thing. It was my guess they wouldn't even be searching the Bradleys' part of the house.

I didn't feel bound by my word to Romano, or

bound to protect his interests. But before anything else happened, I wanted to know what was in this bag. First I had to persuade Casey.

'I think this is what they want,' I told her.

'The bag?'

'Or whatever's inside it.'

'Is it Mano's? Is that what you were to get for him?' She reached for it. I held it back.

'It's locked,' I said.

'Well, we've got one like this. The key may be the same...'

'Where's the key?'

'I don't know. Probably in the kitchen drawer. But we can't...'

'We can't stand here for ever.' I began moving towards the foot of the stairs.

'Jon, why is it all right to go upstairs, and not all right to phone the police?'

I turned round. Nice one. I couldn't think of any good answer. There are times when my brain folds on me. As if somebody cuts the power. I'll be doing something, then for a few seconds I can't remember what I've just done, or what I'm supposed to do next. I can feel it happening, and I can't do a thing about it. This was one of those times. OK, I could have told her all I knew, but I was scared she would panic.

'Well?'

I stared at Humphrey Bogart. He had no ideas either.

'What are you and Mano up to?'

'Nothing.'

'Tell me.'

'I don't know,' I said helplessly.

'Great,' she said tightly. 'All right then. I'm going up.' She took the bag from my unresisting arms, pushed past me and headed for the stairs. 'If they get me, they get me. And it's your fault.'

My fault? Where did she find that idea? I was probably the only innocent character around. Since the first moment I'd got tangled up in this crazy family, I'd been made a fool of, been used, pushed around, and now here I was, trapped in the middle of something that looked distinctly bad. I told myself it was time to get out. Finish. Goodbye. None of my business.

Deaf to my own good advice, I followed her round the house, room by room, which was extremely stupid of us both, being exactly what you're not supposed to do if you think there are burglars around.

It was interesting in a way, getting a quick glimpse of their lifestyle. A musical family, note the piano and guitar case. Old-fashioned parents, judging by their bedroom furniture which was very traditional mahogany. Lovers of foreign parts—on the upper landing there was a skin-covered African shield with crossed spears behind it on the wall, and a massive, coiled, dried snake on the top of the bookcase. It stared at me with cold distrust in its dirty yellow eyes.

Finally, at what I suspected was Casey's bedroom, we collided for the second time that afternoon when she closed the door very rapidly and turned round.

'They're inside?' I breathed.

'No,' she said indignantly.

'Oh. Good.'

'Look, do you have to follow me around like this?'

'I'm following the bag,' I said, trying to lighten the

atmosphere. 'In case your arm gets tired.'

'Have it then.'

I fumbled, let it fall, and it bounced off the banister, plummeting down to the ground floor. There was an ominous crash.

Casey let out a wail and flew down the stairs.

When I got to her, she was on the floor, gathering the pieces of a Chinese-style table lamp that had stood beside the telephone.

'Was it, um . . . valuable?'

She ignored me. For want of anything better to do, I picked up the holdall. One of the seams had split. A slight pull broke a few more stitches. Seeing what was inside, I sat down on the stair and ripped the seam gently till the hole was about three inches long. I drew out a couple of tightly folded small bundles. Ten-pound notes. Prising off the thin rubber band, I did a rapid count. One hundred pounds in the bundle. New notes. So if the bag was full of the same . . .

I looked up. She was staring at the money in my hands. Her eyes met mine.

'Don't ask me, because I don't know,' I said angrily.

'I wasn't going to,' she said quickly.

'Look, none of this is my fault. If you want to blame somebody, blame your friend Romano.' I was feeling more uneasy by the minute. So much money in my hands was unnerving . . .

'He's Bob's friend, not mine.'

'Great. With friends like him, who needs enemies? Al Capone probably had a lot of friends too.'

'Just what are you trying to say? If something's going on around here, I'd like to . . .' Some thought seemed to strike her. 'Wait a minute. When you came to the door that first day, was it Mano you came to see?'

'I didn't know he lived here. I didn't know *who* lived here. Listen, how well do you know him?'

She stared at me, as if she was trying to read my mind, then began, 'Bob met him in first year. He was desperate for somewhere to stay. His parents threw him out because he wanted to be an actor instead of a solicitor. His father's a solicitor.'

'That might come in useful.'

She stiffened. 'You can't mean . . . Mano's not a criminal.'

'So where did all this come from?'

She bit her lip. 'How much do you think . . .'

'A lot,' I interrupted. 'More than part-time waiters earn.'

She was quite still for a couple of seconds, then abruptly she flung the piece of china she was holding at the wall opposite and started to cry.

I admit I felt sick at that point. The guy was so good-looking, I suppose every girl he met fell for him. And the creep knew how to turn on the charm. I guessed she was wishing I would disappear. The story of my life. I should have come into the world fitted with a delete button.

I put the two wads of notes carefully back into the holdall. Half of my brain was saying, 'You've got to get out of this, pal.' The other half was saying, 'How? And what happens to her, if I clear out?' Because even though I didn't have the white horse, the armour or the magic sword, I still had the vague and insane hope that if I hung around long enough, everything could change, and I could get to be the hero.

What were our options? Take the bag to Romano and pretend nothing had happened? Take the bag to the police? And say what? Phone the hospital and see what big brother with the broken nose advised? I sighed and stood up.

'What are you going to do?' She had found a handkerchief and was blowing her nose. Her face was pale, and her eyes still looked watery, but she seemed to have things under control again.

'I don't know. How about a world cruise? Two world cruises.'

'We'd better tell your father.'

'We'll send him a postcard.'

'I meant, we ought to see if he's back. Ask him what to do.'

Introduce Casey to my father at this ultra-delicate stage in our relationship? Beauty and the Beast? The thought made my stomach heave. There had to be another answer.

'He's out most of the day,' I told her.

'Doesn't he have a phone? What do you do if you need him?'

If I needed him? That was the kind of question even Einstein couldn't have answered. I tried another tack.

'You must have some relations.'

'In Cardiff and Ullapool. Couldn't we just go over to your house and wait till he gets back?'

'I don't have a key.'

'So he goes out and you have to wander the streets till he comes home?'

'You had the sheltered childhood, not me.'

That seemed to irritate her.

'You're not even trying, are you? Can't you think of something helpful, instead of making stupid comments? This is serious.'

She was right. And maybe he was better than nothing. A dud parent across the street was worth two in the African bush, or something like that. If he was out, as I thought he would be, we'd lost nothing. Maybe my brain would start functioning better in the open air. I couldn't figure out what was the safest thing to do.

'Please God, show us the right thing to do, in Jesus' name, Amen.'

My jaw dropped. She said defensively, 'I suppose you think it's childish. Praying. That sort of thing.'

'It doesn't bother me,' I said cautiously.

'Even atheists prayed in the trenches.'

How relevant that little gem was in our present dilemma was beyond me, but I muttered something to keep her happy. She ran upstairs to get her purse and jacket. I picked up the holdall again, trying not to wonder exactly how much was in it. Or where it might have come from. Or who might want it back. And how badly.

10

A run with the money

Outside, the bright sunlight seemed wrong. There
should have been heavy fog or even thick mist, to
match how I was feeling. We locked up the house in
silence and we crossed the road in silence. I was
carrying the holdall, wondering how I was going to
explain it.

More important, how was I going to explain Casey
herself, since I'd never mentioned her? I also had a
sick feeling in my insides, imagining what she would
make of my father. He was never drunk, but you could
smell the drink on him like aftershave. I wished now
I'd put her in the picture and told her more about
myself. To me, the man was nothing, but he was going
to be one big disadvantage if I wanted to be anybody
as far as Casey was concerned. Which I did.

It was almost as if she was catching the edges of my
thoughts. As we began to climb my flight of steps, she
said abruptly, 'Did you tell your father Bob knocked
you over the other day?'

'No. I didn't think he'd ...'

'Thank goodness for that. Don't tell him now. I mean I know it was just an accident, but still . . . Colin wanted to come after you, but you'd vanished. He's at the Academy with Bob and Mano but he's studying music.'

'So I heard.'

'Colin's all right,' she added. 'He's actually quite normal compared to them.'

I'd been pressing the bell that would ring outside our door upstairs. To my relief, there was no response. The outer door remained firmly shut.

'Try again,' Casey urged. I did.

'He's out,' I told her, hoping I didn't sound pleased.

'Maybe he's got the TV on. Is your car here?'

An obvious question. In my preoccupied state, it hadn't occurred to me to look up and down the street.

I didn't see his car. What I did see made my stomach go cold.

'Let's go find a police station,' I said rapidly.

'Why? Hey, you don't have to drag me . . .'

'The burglars are back.'

Casey looked behind us, saw two men under a distant lime tree on the far side, saw them begin to move in our direction, and didn't ask questions.

Whatever her faults, that girl could run. She was right beside me all the way round the crescent. We crossed a road, making a white Volkswagen swerve and hoot. Someone was running behind us, but I couldn't tell if he was gaining.

Suddenly she wasn't there. I heard her yell, braked, saw she'd taken a detour into what looked like a disused plumbers' yard, and hurtled after her.

She was clambering over a low wall at the other end. I managed to vault it. The ground on the other side was overgrown with weeds and covered with rubble but then there was a beaten path through some tall trees. I could hear heavy traffic somewhere.

'Here,' she shouted.

We swerved off to the right and moments later I saw a wide dirty brown river. We ran on, dodging round bushes and outstretched roots. I caught sight of the arches of a bridge.

We ran under it. Traffic thundered above our heads. On the other side, two small boys playing with a wet hairy rope jumped up in fright as we careered past.

I saw what she had to be aiming for—a Tube station, right there ahead of us, its walls covered in graffiti but still a beautiful sight—big, solid, full of people. I looked behind for the first time. Nobody. Couldn't be sure though.

She had money for tickets. The air was cold downstairs on the platform. Dirty yellow water lay in pools between the tracks. There was nobody else waiting except two characters in black who looked us over then turned away. I thought the smaller one was female, but it was hard to tell.

'Where are we going?' I asked, once I got my breath back.

'Police station. I think there's one near Cessnock.' Casey scanned the map on the wall. She was wiping sweat off her face with a handkerchief. I used my sleeve.

'Well, you can do the talking,' I told her. 'Why don't we just leave it on the train?'

'Don't be ridiculous. You've got thousands there.'

'Keep your voice down,' I urged her. 'Those two over there could buy a lot of excitement with this little lot.'

She looked at them and shivered. Then she glanced back at the staircase.

'I can't actually believe this is happening. Does this happen to you every time you go on holiday?'

That moment a loud rumble announced a train, orange and black. Soon we were safely inside with the doors closed, rattling along at what felt like sixty but was probably only thirty. We had two companions, a little elderly woman whose feet didn't reach the floor, and a simple-looking boy in a worn brown anorak and jeans. On the roof above the seats opposite, an advert invited me to join the Royal Marine reserves. If I was a young man with courage, initiative and determination, a new world of excitement awaited me. I turned to Casey.

'We have to talk about this some more.'

'Why?'

'Because we don't know for certain . . . what this is,' I ended cryptically. The elderly woman was sitting with gloved hands firmly clamped on her Harrods carrier bag. She'd sniffed both of us over and was carefully looking away, but she was listening all right.

'I don't like being chased. Or burgled,' Casey said hotly.

'Don't talk so loud,' I said a second time. 'What about Romano? We're going to look stupid if this is his. Legally.'

'But they broke into our house . . .'

'Right, but we've lost them. We can't talk about it

here,' I muttered, sensing the ancient ears opposite homing in more and more accurately. Even the boy in the anorak was watching us.

Casey wasn't happy, but she followed me out on to the platform at the next stop, and up into the noisy world of what looked like a main shopping precinct.

'So where should we go?'

'You seem to be making the decisions,' she said shortly.

'You think I'm enjoying this?'

'I don't know.'

'Because I'm not. Any more than you are. I didn't ask to get involved in your crazy family . . .'

She stopped. 'There's nothing wrong with my family. I have a perfectly normal family. Well, maybe not normal, but not what you mean,' she said angrily.

'All right!' I retorted. I dropped the bag on the ground and walked away from it.

'Hey, son, you've dropped yer bag,' a male voice called out, seconds later. A bald, red-faced man bulging out of a white T-shirt had picked up the holdall and was chasing after me. 'You be careful, son,' he warned me earnestly, thrusting it into my arms. 'There's some dirty rascals about these days.'

He rolled away, no doubt feeling like a good citizen. I stood there with the bag in my arms, feeling like I wanted to weep. As I half expected, when I looked round at Casey, her shoulders were shaking.

She came slowly over, trying to pull herself together.

'I'm sorry. I know it's not funny. It was just . . . the look on your face,' she spluttered.

It was infectious. After a few moments, I gave in, and we stood there laughing like a pair of idiots. I threw the bag at her, and she threw it back. Call it a reaction to the previous hour. We laughed till our sides hurt.

'I'm sore,' I told her.

'Me too. Look, we have to do something,' she said, wiping her eyes. 'This is serious.'

We began walking downhill towards the busier part of the street, which was a pedestrian precinct. 'Life Is Serious,' I intoned sternly.

'Well, it is really,' she brushed the hair out of her eyes. 'If we're going to talk, could we sit down somewhere? My ribs are aching.'

There was a stone bench surrounded by massive tubs of white flowers. Two rows of young sycamore trees cast some shade. People of all shapes and sizes swarmed around us in the bright sunlight. The shops were up-market, with well-known names, the same you find in all large towns.

There was a lot of noise. Someone was playing an accordion further down the street, and directly across from us two teenage boys with slicked-back hair, white shirts and ribbon ties were playing guitars while a third in a fifties-style suit sang an old Elvis Presley song. You had to admire his courage. I wondered how much they made in a day. Probably more than you'd think. Enough to make it worthwhile looking ridiculous.

As we watched and listened, an even stranger trio came in sight—three men in dinner suits and huge pink bubble wigs. People on either side were doing a double-take, making sure they'd really seen what they thought they'd seen. Two of the men were carrying long brushes and small black shovels in their white-gloved hands. The third wore a sandwich board over his dinner suit, saying in big black letters, 'Keep Glasgow Tidy'. I was thinking, how much would I need to be paid to put on that outfit, when Casey suddenly shrieked, 'Colin!'

The one wearing the board wheeled round, saw us and instantly registered panic. Casey was already up from the bench and halfway over to him. I didn't move.

11

Caught

I was too far away to hear what Casey was saying, but I could see that Colin's face had gone as pink as his amazing wig. After a few minutes, she turned and gestured for me to come over. I got up with extreme reluctance.

'Tell him I'm not making this up,' she implored me when I reached them. Close-up, the dinner suit was a fraud, a printed T-shirt with long sleeves. The whole costume was obviously somebody's bright idea, to make the populace pay attention and not drop litter. They were certainly paying attention to Colin. The poor guy looked as if he wanted the street to open and swallow him. Embarrassment was flowing from him in hot waves.

'What have you told him?' I asked.

'About the burglars. And Bob's nose. And that,' she pointed nervously at the bag in my arms. 'Talk about coincidence,' she turned to Colin. 'How did you get this job? I couldn't believe my eyes when . . .'

'Casey, I'm supposed to get back to George Square

for the next shift,' Colin interrupted hurriedly. 'I have to catch up with Jack and Trevor. It's bad enough walking in threes ...'

'We'll come with you,' she told him. I quailed inwardly.

'I don't think that's a good idea. Look, let me know what happens, OK? I have to get this stuff back. Tell Bob to take it easy, OK? Tell him I'll phone.'

With that he moved away as fast as the board allowed.

We went back to the bench. Casey looked grim.

'Come on. What did you actually expect him to do?' I said after a moment or two.

'Something helpful?' she said tightly.

'In that outfit?' I still felt embarrassed for the poor guy.

She bit her lip. 'He could have.'

'You really think so?'

'You said it this morning,' she began, after an interval. 'People aren't there when you need them.'

'Did I say that?'

'They just aren't there,' she said, spacing the words.

I wanted to point out that I was there. Didn't I count? Was I invisible or something?

'Maybe I am naive. Immature. I didn't think I was. But maybe I am.'

'Don't let it bother you.'

She ignored me. 'I don't know,' she said wearily. 'I suppose I just expect people to be honest and kind and ... and nice to me. I know in my head that they won't be, not always, not the way the world is. I know what goes on. I mean, I watch the news like everybody else. I know all that. So what's wrong with me? Why should it surprise me when it happens?'

Since I wasn't sure what she was getting at, I stayed dumb.

'But some people are naturally kind,' she went on, 'even though they don't have any room for God in their lives. Like you. You're a nice person.'

'Am I?' I was visible again. I wasn't sure I wanted to be, the way the conversation now seemed to be going...

'Yes, you are. You brought the lamb chops back. And you didn't need to help when Bob fell. You...'

'Casey, not all the atheists prayed in the trenches.'

She digested that for a few seconds then said, 'You told me you just looked like a rebel.'

'Sometimes I tell lies.'

She fell silent.

I stared at the people passing, cursing inwardly. What was I playing at? What did I want? If I was honest with myself, the bottom line was, I wanted her to think I was wonderful. But I wanted her to take it for granted. No true confessions. And no probing. I had to stay intact, behind the Joe Cool front.

Every girl in school at home knew exactly who I was. Most of them had known for years. I was the one who'd come bottom in every spelling test in junior school, who still couldn't get his tie done fast enough after P.E., who got lost orienteering round the sports field, because he couldn't tell left from right. Being good at Maths put the tin lid on it. What normal person ever enjoyed Maths?

Then I looked at Casey, and something inside me crumpled. One minute I was sure of myself, and the next I was lost. I was tired of acting. I didn't want to pretend with Casey. Even if it meant the end.

'Casey, I am not a nice person. If you'd been fat and ugly, I would have left Bob lying on the path.'

She looked up, brushing back that amazing shiny hair. Then she said slowly, 'If you'd been fat and ugly, I wouldn't have asked you to come in the ambulance.'

That kind of silenced me. I was scared to make too much of it. Finally, I took refuge in a joke.

'And I thought you were only after my money.'

As soon as the words left my lips we both remembered. We stared at the bag on my knee. How could we have forgotten? Seconds ticked away like a bomb. At last she stood up.

'Let's phone Romano,' she said bleakly.

'And?'

'See what he says,' she suggested helplessly.

We'd passed two phone boxes just at the top of the Underground steps, but there was a queue waiting for them, so we wandered back along the street till we came to a coffee shop, where Casey said there was a pay phone.

Nobody was using it, but before we could, a manageress-type woman appeared.

'I'm sorry, this is just for the use of customers,' she said shortly. Her lipstick was the colour of overripe strawberries.

'We're customers,' I told her.

'Then perhaps you could give the waitress your order?' She smiled with no warmth. 'There's a table by the window.'

'Have you any money left?' I muttered to Casey, as we slid into the seats. She checked her purse then glanced at the menu.

'Enough for a phone call, one black coffee and two straws. Unless we walk home.'

I looked back at the manageress, who was turning her charm on a portly, middle-aged man in a dark suit. 'We could always use some of this,' I tapped the holdall.

Before Casey could squash my suggestion, the waitress was upon us, small and thin, and far too tired to smile at us.

'Two glasses of mineral water, please,' I said quickly, and to my relief she jotted that down and turned away.

'Mineral water costs more than apple juice,' Casey said worriedly, scanning the card.

'Never mind that. Let's do what we came for,' I told her impatiently.

We had to use the directory again. Once the phone started ringing, Casey for some reason handed me the receiver. I asked for Romano. A female voice said he was busy. I told her it was life or death and said I wasn't joking. I waited, watching the digital figures ticking away. Casey had put in a pound coin. I hoped it was going to be enough.

At last he came. He began to speak but I cut in, 'Listen, we've got your bag, and we know what's in it.'

'Who is this?' he said angrily.

'Jon Moore. You told me to get it, remember? Casey's here with me. We're in a pay phone.'

I think he swore in Italian. Somebody else was talking to him, probably telling him to get back to work.

'Where are you?' he asked.

'Where are we?' I turned to Casey. She told me and I passed on the information.

'Stay there,' he told me. 'Stay exactly where you are and don't move. Is that clear?'

'Casey wants to go to the police. That man I was telling . . .'

'Is she with you?'

'I just said so.'

There was another outburst in Italian. It sounded as if he was ready to break something, possibly me. He said once again, 'Don't move from there,' then hung up.

'Well?' Casey asked.

'He's coming here.'

We moved back to the table. Two glasses and two bottles of mineral water were waiting for us.

'What's wrong now?' Casey asked, reading my face.

'He's angry. He told me not to get you involved.'

'That was thoughtful of him. Pity he didn't tell the burglars.' She poured some water into her glass then wrinkled her nose at it. 'I don't even like this stuff. It makes me burp.'

'Then don't drink it.'

She smiled, as if the idea hadn't occurred to her.

'Do you ever do things you don't want to do?'

'Sure. I'm doing it.'

She looked hurt, as if I meant being with her. I said quickly, 'Not this. I meant being on holiday with my father.'

She was playing with her bottle cap, pushing it round and round the table. It skipped over to me, and I flicked it back.

'Why is that so bad?' she asked.

'Because I don't like him, and he doesn't like me.'

'Then why are you having a holiday together?'

'You tell me. My grandmother thought it was a good idea. He's been away a long time.' I trapped the bottle cap before it fell off the side. 'I had a job lined up down at the boat-yard, but they couldn't afford to take me on this year.'

'So what would you be doing right now? If you were at home.'

'If I wasn't at the yard? Keeping out of my grandmother's way.'

'Doing what?' she persisted.

I had to think about it.

'I'd be sitting on the shingle at the end of Arthur's Marsh, watching the sea.'

She made a funny little grimace, which could have meant anything. We sat in silence for a while after that. I think we were both feeling the same. We'd coped so far, just, but now things were coming to a head and we were both nervous, hating the thought of what was going to happen when Romano arrived. I drank my mineral water and she left hers after a couple of sips. Then two women with a lot of shopping sat down at our table. Despite the No Smoking signs, one of them lit up.

'Let's go,' I mouthed to Casey, and she nodded.

After she'd paid the bill, we had less than fifty pence left.

'Maybe it would be better if you went home,' I suggested, as we made our way outside.

'No, I want to speak to him.'

'But he's mad at me for getting you into this.

Whatever it is.'

'I'm mad at him. He'd better have some good explanations.'

Maybe we were both tired. Or else it was just standing there against the plate glass in the sun and the noise, but we saw nothing until it was too late.

I heard Casey gasp. A man in a white sweatshirt had her by the arm. I whirled round, to face the man in the brown leather jacket.

'OK, pal,' he smiled at me. 'No nonsense this time.'

12

A stupid move

Casey yelled, 'Help! Police! Police!'

People stopped, heads turned, a couple of figures began to move our way, then the white-sweatshirted one called out, 'Keep calm, everybody, this is the police.'

They were. They had their warrant cards out already, if we'd been bright enough to notice. They walked us quite rapidly to the edge of the pedestrian precinct where the dark-blue Sierra was waiting, its radio cackling cryptically to itself.

I think Casey was crying on the way to the police station, but since she was in the back and I'd been put in the front, I couldn't see. Or talk to her.

They kept us apart when we got to the station too. I had to sign a form, saying I was there voluntarily. Then I sat with a silent constable for a long, long time. The holdall had, of course, been taken from me right at the start. Eventually the door to my cosy little chamber opened and the man in the leather jacket came in. The constable stopped lounging and stood up straight against the wall.

'Right, son,' he began, 'I'm Detective Inspector McGuigan and you're Jonathan Moore. Let's have it.' He sounded bored, as if he'd been dealing with delinquent teenagers for at least a hundred years. I was just the next in line.

'Am I allowed to ask questions?'

He looked amused. 'Mebbe. Mebbe not.'

'Are the police allowed to break into people's houses?'

'With a search warrant, in hot pursuit, they are.'

'Why didn't you ring the doorbell?'

'We did, and we battered on the door. We also tried the side door. Where were you anyway?'

'In a cupboard. It looks like part of the wall.'

'We'll have to go back and look for it.' He leaned forward. 'So tell me, what were you thinkin' of doin' wi' your parcel?'

There didn't seem much point in telling him anything other than the truth, even if the truth made no sense, so I told him everything. How I'd seen him in the street, how I'd told Romano, how Romano had told me to get the holdall and bring it to him.

'So what stopped you?'

That was harder to explain. I wondered what Casey was telling them. She'd wanted to go to the police all along, but I'd argued against it. She was so keen on doing the right thing. I remembered how she'd prayed out loud. She was the type who would never dream of breaking even the most pointless of school rules, and now here she was in a police station, and it was my fault . . .

'Ah'm waitin',' he said heavily.

'The bag got burst by accident. Once we saw what was in it, we . . . well, we didn't know what to do. That was after you'd searched the room. We thought you were the bad guys. But we didn't know you wanted the money. Except we didn't know then it was money . . . not until it burst.'

It sounded incoherent, even to me, and I knew what I was trying to say. Also my head was feeling the way your head does when your stomach is loudly telling you it's food and drink time, so I was not at my sparkling best.

Inspector McGuigan pushed his hand over his cropped sandy hair. He looked frustrated. And hot. He'd slung his jacket over the back of the chair while I'd been talking, and I could see dark patches of sweat marking his shirt under the arms.

I followed his glance and swivelled round. It seemed like the silent constable had been taking notes.

'What's the matter?'

'What's he writing? Am I making a statement?' I said edgily.

'No, you're not. I've just got a lousy memory. Keep going.'

'I should have an adult here,' I protested. 'You can't write things down unless you tell me you're going to. And you're supposed to record it on tape.'

'Here's another one seen the film,' he said sarcastically. He gestured at me with an accusing finger. 'You're sixteen years and two months, pal, you're the adult.' He hit the table and leaned forward. 'You've wasted enough of my time today. You left the house. Then what?'

I didn't like the look in his eyes. I stumbled on. Repeating myself, groping for the right word. I sounded like someone whose native language was Serbian. Then when I said we'd tried to get hold of my father, he wanted to know what his business was, and why we were in Scotland, and we got into a long, dismal sidetrack, with lots of questions on his part and precious few answers on mine.

He obviously thought I was trying to hide something, but what else could I tell him? When I staggered to a final halt, he looked totally dissatisfied. He made a noise in the back of his throat, like a snort of mingled disbelief and anger. As if he'd never had to deal with anyone this stupid.

I'd seen that expression too often in too many classrooms. I lost my grip. I'd been fingering the coil of wire in my pocket. Now I pulled it out.

'You can have this back,' I said.

'Where did you find it?' he answered. His expression didn't change.

'On the rosebush.'

He thought about that, then nodded slowly, 'Of course.'

'He only broke his nose, not his neck. So it did work. Except it was Bob, not Romano. Of course it could have been Casey.'

'Who's Casey?'

'Hope Bradley. It's a nickname. She could have been the first to come down the steps.'

I was angry, and he must have known it, but it made no difference. I waited for some faint hint of remorse to shadow his face, but he didn't react. Well trained, I supposed. When I'd started speaking, a little voice in my head had protested that I was out of line, that policemen didn't set up booby traps, that I was creating trouble for myself, but this careful lack of reaction convinced me that he'd done it all right. I couldn't think why, but he'd done it.

Then I had a sudden image of Casey with her face smashed, and I felt sick. I wanted to know that she was OK. I wanted to get out of this place, away from him.

'How long have we got to stay here?'

He ignored the question. He picked up the wire and tested it against his thumb. Then he stood up. 'Don't go away,' he said absently. As if I had a choice . . .

The door closed behind him. In the silence that remained, slowly the feeling grew in me that I'd done something very stupid. That piece of wire was evidence against him and now he had it.

Who would believe me? Who'd believe a policeman would set up something so crude? I'd not have believed it if I hadn't seen it. I glanced over at the uniformed man, but he avoided my eye. It wasn't worth wondering whose side he'd be on.

13

A deafening silence

After what seemed like ages, the door was opened by a sergeant. He was tall and bald and smelled of the same awful pipe tobacco my grandfather used.

'Out you come, lad,' he said placidly.

'What for?'

'You don't want to stay all night, do you?' he asked and laughed at his own joke. 'The food here's terrible. Right, Alan?'

The constable rose and stretched himself, muttering something inaudible.

I followed the bald sergeant through the corridor into a wider one. Casey was standing there, with the other detective, a middle-aged couple, and Romano. The woman was overweight but still good-looking, well-dressed, with plenty of gold draped round her neck and weighing down her ear lobes. She was holding Romano's arm and talking to him urgently. He met my eye and lifted his eyebrows, as if we were fellow sufferers. I didn't respond.

The man in the immaculate dark suit had to be his

father. A couple of inches shorter, hairline in retreat and waistline advancing a little, but with the same tanned handsome face. The detective in the white sweatshirt was listening to him impassively, arms folded.

Casey smiled at me weakly then looked at the floor. The man in the prosperous suit turned and caught sight of me.

'This is the boy? Jonathan, isn't it?' He reached out and grasped my hand. I was drawn forward into the group. His arm went round my shoulders, in an unavoidable hug. The plump woman let go of Romano, and for a terrible moment I thought she was going to fall on me and kiss me, but I escaped with another handshake.

'You poor boy!' she exclaimed, in a heavy Italian accent, 'Your mother must be worried out of her mind about you. And so far from home! You must be worn out with all this terrible business. Oh, you children, what you do to us!'

I got my hand back, slightly crushed. The detective behind us said drily, 'Right sir, I think that's about all for now. If you don't mind. We'll be in touch.'

Then, astonishingly, we were outside in the street. Free as the air, which was now a lot cooler, and sweeter than any city air I'd ever breathed.

Romano's father began organizing everybody towards the car park at the far end of the building. Casey still wasn't looking at me, and I couldn't think of a way to start a conversation. Actually I could think of at least a half dozen, but when I tried them inside my head they all sounded banal. I suppose everyone assumed I knew what was happening. Maybe I didn't look as bewildered as I felt.

Without asking questions, I got into the front seat of a red Alfa Romeo when the door was opened for me. Moments later, Romano got into the driver's seat. I turned round, to see Casey in the back, leaning limply in the corner. She looked as if she'd been crying. Out of the corner of my eye I saw the man and the woman drive off in a very smooth Mercedes. Romano spoke first.

'OK, we've got wheels. Where do we want to go?'

'Nowhere with you,' I said. How could he talk to us like this, as if he'd done nothing wrong? I couldn't believe it. His nerve took my breath away.

He sat without replying for a few seconds, then he switched off the engine, pulled out the key and threw it in my lap.

'What's this for?'

'You take her home. I'll take a bus.' he said, opening his door a fraction.

'You know I can't drive,' I said, doubly angry. I saw what he was doing. He was the one who'd caused all our trouble, and now, instead of apologizing or explaining, he was fooling about, making me look stupid in front of Casey.

I sensed her stirring in the back of the car.

'Jon, please . . .' she began.

He swivelled round to face me. 'See?' his hands gestured towards Casey, 'You're upsetting her. Why don't you just . . .'

'Why don't you tell me what the heck's been happening!'

'Give me a chance, pal. I . . .'

'And you can have these,' I flung the keys back at

him, more violently than I meant to. They caught him on the side of the face.

I tensed. Now I was in trouble.

With one hand still on his cheek, he said slowly, 'You want to settle this somewhere else?'

'If you want to.'

What was I talking like this for? He was taller, heavier, older. I'd never been in a fight, not a proper one. The odd playground scuffle, before the teachers came out yelling, that didn't count . . .

'If you like,' I repeated diffidently, while my brain scrabbled around frantically, like a flea-bitten mongrel in a box. Should I talk some more? Should I get out and run now? Or wait till he was getting out of his side of the car, and gain a couple of seconds? But where would I run to? I didn't even know where I was.

'You know what I would like?' Casey spoke up from the depths of the back seat. 'If anybody was interested. I would like a bag of chips. And a can of Coke. If anybody had the money.'

Romano looked at her, then back at me, then abruptly burst out laughing. He started the car. We pulled slowly out into the street. I saw that the skin on his cheek wasn't broken, just bruised, but it looked sore. I didn't feel safe yet, despite the laughter.

'Those were my parents,' he began, not looking at me but concentrating on the traffic, 'and this is the mama car. A symbol of my acceptance back into the bosom of the family. One repentant phone call from the prodigal, and the old folks came rallying round like I'd never been away. And thanks to my highly respected legal genius of a father, we're let loose on the unsuspecting public once more.'

It didn't sound all that reassuring. Just how much had he known about the money? Where was the truth in all of this?

I thought about my father. Even if I was technically an adult, it stood to reason the police would be round sooner or later to let him know what I'd been up to. Would he blow me apart or shrug his shoulders? He had a low opinion of the police, but that didn't mean he'd approve of what I'd been doing.

For a couple of seconds I let myself wonder what it would be like to have a father who got things done, as Romano's father had. Someone with influence. Someone other people had to respect.

With my father I had the strange sensation most of the time that there was something different going on inside his head. As if he was hearing voices, like those guys on chat shows who're talking to the audience while another voice sends secret messages through the hidden mike.

Or was it just me? Maybe I bored him. I didn't sparkle the way the ideal son should. Well, too bad. I wasn't that bothered. I wasn't repentant either.

Romano swerved into the outside lane just as the traffic lights ahead changed to red. 'So you want to know what's happening?' he went on. 'What's happening is, my sweet cousin Tony set me up. He gave me some of his stuff last month, compact discs, portable TV... Said he didn't want to leave it in his flat while he was away. He let me think that bag was home videos. You know what I mean.' His voice dropped, too low for Casey. 'You know the kind of stuff...'

'And you didn't look?' I said sceptically, not

believing a word of it. His tone was just too frank and friendly.

'No, I didn't.' He jerked the car into gear and we swung round the corner. Casey cried out in protest at the sudden burst of speed, and he said, 'OK, OK,' and slowed a little.

'But you must have known those guys were the police,' I said, growing more irritated the more I thought about it. 'You let us think they were crooks. You made us look like idiots. There we were, scared out of our skulls, running across half the city . . .'

'OK, I'm sorry,' he said heavily. 'I got it wrong. I thought if I didn't look, it didn't matter. Then when you said McGuigan had been watching the flat, I panicked. The way I looked at it, the less you knew the better. And anyway, I didn't want Casey involved. But then they came to the restaurant when you ran off, in case I knew where you'd head for. I admitted you were bringing the bag to me. They were right beside me when you phoned again. They said, tell them to stay put . . .'

'So they could pick us up like criminals,' I said angrily. 'You should have phoned them at the start . . .'

'Look, I was only guessing. I didn't know till half an hour ago what was in the bag.'

'Who told them you had it?'

'Could be one of his pals. His ex-pals. Your guess is as good as mine. He said he was going to Milan, but who knows where he is. I know where I'd like to put him. He's always been a spam heid, but he's never done anything this stupid before. It never occurred . . .'

'What exactly has he done?' Casey interrupted.

'You tell me,' Romano said tersely. He was driving very slowly now, evidently watching for a parking space at the side of the road. 'Nobody at the police station was giving much away, not even to Dad. Something highly illegal, that's for sure. Nobody prints their own banknotes for a hobby.'

'You mean they were forged? They weren't real?' Casey and I spoke in unison.

Without replying, he put the car into reverse and began manoeuvring into a gap next to a ramshackle-looking shop, with 'Rocky's Fish and Chips' in fluorescent red above the door. Two boys with bikes were leaning against the wall, eating chips with their fingers. They looked at the car and exchanged comments.

Romano pulled out some notes from his pocket.

'Here. This stuff's real.' He tossed a couple of fivers on to my knee. 'You go with him, flower,' he told Casey. 'They won't understand his accent. Get me a fish supper. No vinegar.'

'Aren't you coming?' she asked.

'I'll stay with the transport. Wheel trims are very collectable round here.'

'How do we know you won't just drive away?' I said.

'You don't,' he smiled at me. 'You're going to have to trust me.'

There were three people ahead of us in the queue. Two men in dirty white overalls splashed with paint, and an unbelievable middle-aged woman with dyed black hair. She looked twenty from the back, and fifty plus from the front.

'What do you want?' Casey asked me.

'I don't know.' I tried without success to read the list on the back wall. It was handwritten in small sloping letters. 'Just chips,' I muttered.

'Have something else. He's paying.'

'I don't want anything else.'

She bit her lip and looked away. Nothing more was said. Our turn came. She ordered two fish suppers and separate chips for me and was told we'd have to wait for the fish. Not long, the man assured us. We stood against the end of the counter beside a tall but wilting rubber plant. A scruffy girl of about seven with an even smaller sister came in and bought a loaf of bread and two cartons of milk. She elbowed her way out through the door as if she'd done it many times before.

'Jonathan, I'm sorry.'

I looked at Casey in surprise. What did she have to be sorry for?

'Don't be mad at me,' she said quietly.

'I'm not mad at you.'

'You sound mad.'

'I'm not. I'm just tired.' It was the truth, if not the whole truth. It wasn't her I was mad at. I was sure Romano was lying through his teeth, but there was no way I could prove it. And it looked as if Casey believed him. That was the worst part. If I said anything against him, it would sound like jealousy, as if I felt inferior to him. Which in a way was true, because I did envy him, even though I hated his guts. It was pulling me down to the ground.

'I'm just tired,' I repeated.

She smiled weakly. 'Me too. I just want to lie down and sleep for a month. When Mr and Mrs Cardosi came in, I just collapsed.'

I glanced out to where Romano sat in the car. I wished I'd had the courage to take him on. And the muscles. He'd known I wasn't wanting a fight. He'd be laughing at me for a million years.

'Casey, do you think he's telling the truth? About the money?'

'Why wouldn't he be? I wish you two would stop sniping at one another. We were never in any real danger, and it's all over now, and we . . .'

'You make it sound as if he didn't do anything.'

'But he didn't really. It was his cousin's fault. And we didn't do anything wrong either. Those policemen could have shouted, told us who they were . . .'

'I suppose they thought they'd outrun us.'

'Well, I couldn't do it again tonight. After I've had this fish supper, I just want to fall down in a quiet heap. I might not get up tomorrow at all . . . What's the matter?'

'I was thinking about your brother,' I said reluctantly. Her words had triggered off the memory of his fall.

'Oh help,' she caught hold of her hair. 'That's incredible. I'd forgotten.'

From behind the counter the grey-haired man called out, 'Youse wantin' salt and vinegar on yer suppers, hen?'

Casey said 'yes' to salt, 'no' to vinegar, and took the parcel of food. I handed over the money and pocketed the change. As soon as we were in the car she said, 'Mano, I have to see Bob. Can we go to the hospital?'

'Before or after we eat these?' he asked.

'We'll eat them on the way.'

'I can't change gear with a piece of haddock in my hand, petal. Just keep them wrapped. We'll eat in the hospital car park.' He revved the engine to scare the boys who were now fooling about near the car. They scattered.

'What do you want to do?' He glanced at me as we pulled out into the traffic. 'You want to come to the hospital with us?'

It hadn't occurred to me that I would do anything else. I waited for Casey to state the obvious, to say, 'Of course he's coming,' or words to that effect.

She didn't. And with Romano there, there was no way I could ask her whether she wanted me to come or not. I couldn't even turn round to read her eyes. Why didn't she speak?

'OK, we'll be at the end of the road soon. I can drop you off,' he suggested affably.

I suppose I'd asked for it. I'd told him I didn't want to go anywhere in a car he was driving. The silence in the back seat was deafening. Don't call us, we'll call you.

I said that was fine, which it wasn't. In no time at all we'd stopped, and I was getting out and Casey was calling at me and handing me a bag of chips through the window.

I watched the car disappear. There was a beige and blue litter bin stuck on a lamp post beside me. I dumped the chips in it and walked away.

14

Time to let go

It was a lovely evening. A cheerful blonde woman in navy shorts told me so when she overtook me, her black and white King Charles spaniel straining on its lead. Two young girls cycled by, off the saddles and pushing hard to keep up their speed on the slope, tennis rackets sticking out of their backpacks. A lovely July evening, lovely for tennis or walking the dog. Lovely.

I tried to persuade myself that nothing had seriously changed. I could knock on Casey's door the following day and ask how Bob was. I *could* do that. But I knew I wouldn't.

I wondered when the police would come knocking on our door. My pace slowed. It was nearly eight o'clock. I'd been out of the house since before noon. What kind of explanation was I going to produce? Well, no, nothing much happened while you were out. I went to hospital in an ambulance with this boy I hardly know, then his house got burgled, except it didn't, and I ran across the city with his sister and thousands in forged notes and didn't quite get arrested. Then this other boy nearly beat me up and I lost the girl at the end. Nothing of any importance.

'Hey!' a voice broke into my misery. I looked round.

Colin, in denim cut-offs and a striped shirt with the sleeves rolled up, was cycling across the street towards me. For a violinist, he'd have made a good scrum half. I stopped reluctantly.

'I just tried the Bradleys',' he announced. 'Where is everybody? Have you seen them?'

'She's at the hospital. Romano took her.'

His mouth fell open. 'You mean ... Bob did get hurt?'

'He broke his nose. Casey told you.'

He let out a heavy sigh then wiped sweat off his upper lip with the back of one hand. 'I thought she was putting me on. Hey, wait a minute,' he called as I moved away. 'What happened? Where is he? Which hospital?'

'I don't know,' I said, still backing off. 'The one her father works in.'

He began cycling, keeping beside me, though it meant he was right in the gutter, close to the parked cars.

'How bad is he? I feel terrible. Poor kid, I honestly thought she was ... I mean it sounded like she was making it up as she went along. I thought she was just talking to keep me standing there so I'd have to ... Hey, what was all that stuff she was saying about Mano?' he added.

'Get her to tell you.'

We were at the gate that led to our rented flat.

'Are you OK?' he asked. 'You look as if somebody stole your scone.'

'My what?' He was really beginning to annoy me. Why didn't he ride off into the sunset?

'Just a phrase. My granny used to say it all the time. Here,' he added abruptly, digging into his back pocket. My first thought was that he was offering me money. I drew back.

'Here, have these,' he held out a couple of bits of card.

I took them gingerly.

'It's tomorrow. Lunchtime concert. I'm at the back. Second violins. Gregor Sutherland's the soloist, so it'll be worth hearing. Bob won't be going, but Casey still might, I suppose,' he said, more to himself than to me. 'I've just put some extra tickets through their door,' he explained. 'They'd promised to help with the lunch. No, I'm giving them to you,' he added, as I made to give him the tickets back, having seen the price at the bottom.

'It's not my kind of thing,' I told him.

'You might enjoy it. It's all pretty light stuff. And the food's supposed to be lavish.'

I guessed he was trying to ease his conscience.

'So what do you wear for this? The penguin outfit?'

He laughed ruefully. 'Don't rub it in. I didn't think anyone would recognize me. Everybody thinks I'm working for the Parks Department. Which is true. But the money's good and sheet music costs a bomb. I'm never going to hear the end of it now,' he smiled broadly.

Under normal circumstances I might have liked him, but right now my ego was raw and bleeding. He looked as if he could cope with life pretty easily, manoeuvring his way through it effortlessly with one hand the way he manoeuvred the bike. All his problems were temporary, whereas mine stretched out ahead of me for ever, on a dismal road going nowhere.

He was looking at his watch.

'I might just make visiting. See you around. Maybe tomorrow, if you change your mind, OK?'

Adjusting his gears, and with a quick glance behind, he pulled out into the road and was soon out of sight. I was tempted to drop the tickets in the gutter, but I stuck them in my pocket instead.

I turned to look up at the window. My father was standing there watching me.

I laid a bet with myself and won. His first words were, predictably, 'Where have you been?' then, 'Who was that boy?'

I went over to the sink and poured myself a glass of cold water.

'I'm waiting for an answer, Jonathan.'

He was holding on to the back of a chair as if to steady himself. Warning bells began ringing in my brain. My body went cold, as if the water had flooded the whole of my insides. He must have been knocking it back for hours to get like this. Every drunk was unpredictable; and he was unpredictable sober.

I moved as undeliberately as I could towards the hall door, but he blocked me.

'I'm waiting for an answer,' he said again.

'Nowhere special. I had a look round the shops.'

'Shops closed three hours ago. Who was that on the bicycle? What did he want? What'd you tell him about me?' The words slurred into one another.

'He was selling tickets for a concert,' I said, trying again to edge past.

To my utter astonishment, a hand came up and whammed me across the mouth. Something hard, his signet ring, it must have been, split open my bottom lip. I fell back against the sink. My elbow caught the glass of water. It toppled over on to the floor and shattered. I hung there, stunned, disbelieving, feeling my lip swell, dribbling blood and saliva.

He stared at me for a couple of seconds, then his hands came up, slowly, as if he was pleading.

'Jonny, I'm sorry. I'm sorry, son. I didn't mean it.' He passed a hand over the thin strands of brown hair on his scalp, swayed, steadied himself and came forward, getting me by the shoulders before I could avoid him.

'I'm not a well man, Jonny. Shouldn't have done that. You're my boy, shouldn't do that to my boy.'

I turned my face from him. He went on remorselessly, 'I've not been well, that's the problem. Not been well. But I'll be better soon. Got everything. Got all I need. Then she'll go away, Johnny, she'll go away. She'll rest in peace. Told me she would, you see, she told me that. We'll be all right. We'll do things, you and me.' He patted me gently on the side of the face. 'Jonny. Don't you worry. Hear me? You hear me?'

'I hear you,' I said helplessly. I straightened up, trying to pull away, but he grasped me, pulling me to him. We stayed locked in that unholy embrace for several minutes. I was facing the TV. It was spewing out canned laughter every twenty seconds in some unfunny sitcom. I closed my eyes and the laughter seemed to get even louder.

When he finally let me go, his eyes were wet with emotion.

'You're a good boy,' he told me. 'Got your mother's face. Blue eyes...'

Mumbling some more about my late mother, he stumbled sideways into one of the armchairs. Wasting no time, I made for my own room. Inside, I wedged a chair against the handle. There was no lock. I tried to move the chest of drawers, but it was an ancient, heavy wooden affair, and wouldn't budge.

I was shaking, and I felt sick. I moved to the window and leaned my face against the cool glass. All sorts of desperate ideas were dancing in my brain. Was he often this bad, or was it just because I'd been out too long? I couldn't stay with him now. I couldn't stand him. But how could I get back home? I'd no money, apart from Romano's small change in my pocket—enough for some food but not for a bus or a train. I'd have to hitch a ride.

I stood there for ages, expecting him to try the door. Then I realized I was tensing every time a car entered the crescent, in case it would be Romano's, or even when the colour was wrong, in case it would stop at the Bradleys' anyway. None did.

I asked myself what difference it would have made in any case. Casey hadn't needed me, not me personally. I could see that now. It was just that I'd been there. Anyone would have done. Now I'd faded from the scene. Romano Cardosi was too old for Casey, but she wouldn't see it that way. He had the looks and the tan and the fast car. All I had was a burst lip and a crushed ego. I told myself that both would heal, that it was time to let go.

But I couldn't. When I lay on the bed and closed my eyes, all I could see was Casey in that yellow sweatshirt, bright as the sea poppies on the edge of Arthur's Marsh. I didn't want her in my mind but she was there. The unfairness of it all caught at my chest like a blow.

'Can you hear me, God?' I said angrily. 'If you're there, which I doubt. But just in case you are listening in somewhere, I want you to know . . .'

This was insane. What point was there in being angry with a God I didn't believe in? That was the one thing that annoyed me about Casey. But it wasn't her fault. They'd brought her up like that. And it must have been easy to accept everything. Easy for Casey, with doting parents, and a big brother to fight her battles, and the big house, and a life smooth as milk. Some day she'd know better, I thought bitterly.

I wallowed in the muddy satisfaction of that thought for a few minutes, then suddenly I saw that that wasn't what I wanted at all. She was open and honest, and she really thought there was a benevolent Someone in charge, and something in me wanted her always to have that, even if I couldn't.

'You better look after her,' I told the God I didn't believe in. 'You better take really good care of her, OK?'

I lay there for a while, trying to make sense out of all that had happened. My mouth was sore, and so was my head, but that was probably just hunger, and there was no way I was going out of the room tonight. Finally I decided that in the morning I would pack my stuff and leave. I hoped I could hitch rides, but I was going back down south, even if I had to walk the whole way.

In my mind I took myself down the track from the village, out along the road, past the windmill, and down on to the marsh. I sat high up on the shingle and watched the blue-grey waves crash against the shore till I fell asleep.

15

More of McGuigan

In the middle of the night, I woke up feeling lousy. I had to eat, but first I wanted to clean my face. Without putting any lights on, I felt my way to the bathroom. Locking the door, I inspected my mouth in the glare of the shaving strip light. It looked worse than it felt. I'd made a mistake not putting cold water on it right away.

Through in the dark again, I found the fridge and got hold of the cheese and the margarine. A knife and the remains of a loaf completed my haul. Then I had to come back for a carton of milk. I didn't bother with a cup. I ate very carefully, cutting the cheese into small thin strips, the bread likewise, and dropping them in, trying not to touch my bottom lip. Pantomime stuff. It reminded me of the one time I'd had a tooth filled, and the dentist's dire warning, 'Don't eat your lips tonight,' when the injection made them feel like rubber.

It took me a long time to get back to sleep, so it wasn't surprising that it was midmorning before I woke. I wasn't too worried. Packing didn't take long and I was sure, once I thought rationally about it, that my father would still be unconscious after last night's performance. I didn't leave a message. Let him work it out, I thought, if and when he's sober enough.

It was a grey morning, but the air was heavy. I couldn't stop myself looking over at the Bradleys', but there was nothing to see. Up in the small second floor window, which I knew belonged to Casey's room, the curtains were drawn back, but even that told me nothing. No milk at the door. Well, maybe they didn't have their milk delivered. It was pointless. I was only wasting time.

I'd almost reached the main road when I heard my name being called. I looked round and saw with a sinking heart that it was Detective Inspector McGuigan, leaning on the opened window of the familiar dark-blue Sierra. 'Come here,' he called shortly. 'I want you.'

I crossed the road. He was on his own and he motioned to me to get in at the passenger side. I hesitated, but he made the instruction more emphatic. I opened the door and began to sit, but then I didn't know what to do with the rucksack.

'Put that in the back,' he said irritably, as I tried to wedge myself and the bag in.

His questions were more or less the same as they'd been the night before. Why was I here in Glasgow? How well did I know the Bradleys? Why had I gone to the restaurant that first day? Etc., etc. I stuck to my story, feeble as it was. I didn't like him or his button down shirts, or his aftershave, but I tried not to let it show. He'd have to accept my story sooner or later. It wasn't as if I was holding back vital information. He knew more than I did about what had been going on.

'Which lamp post was it, then?' he said after some seconds of silence, during which he'd been looking out at the street.

'What?'

'The one you walked into.'

I couldn't think of a reply.

'Or was it Cardosi? You looked as if you might've had one or two wee matters to discuss wi' him.'

'I haven't seen him,' I said.

'You left together,' he retorted accusingly.

'I've told you all I know,' I said desperately, unsettled by the quick memory of how close I'd come to making a fool of myself in just the way McGuigan suspected. 'What do you want from me? You got the money back and you probably know who took it. I mean, you know more than me.'

'You think so?'

'Who told you the money was in the Bradleys' house anyway?'

'The usual. Anonymous phone call. Your father home this morning?' he added.

'Could be.'

'I was thinking of having a word wi' him.'

'Feel free.'

Either my voice gave me away, or else there was something in my face. His eyes narrowed.

'So. It was him then, was it? Belted ye one, did he? Very nice.'

I stared fixedly at the grey plastic dashboard.

'Very nice. I think we'll definitely have a word. Big man, is he? Athletic type?'

When I said nothing, he made a noise that sounded like a snort of disgust then said, 'All right, you can go. But don't lose yerself. I've no' finished wi' you yet. What's in that thing?' he added sharply as I twisted round to heave my bag over. 'Where are you off to?'

'Dirty washing,' I said quickly.

'And the rest of the day? Just in case I want you.'

My hand was in my pocket. I pulled out the tickets Colin had given me.

'I'm going to this,' I told him, showing him one of the cards.

He looked at me, at the ticket again, and I knew exactly what he was thinking. 'Go for this kind of stuff, do you?'

I gave him the only classical music fact I knew, mimicking Colin, oozing sincerity. 'Gregor Sutherland's the soloist, so it should be good.'

McGuigan glanced at the card again. 'You're going to be late. It starts in ten minutes. It'll be over by the time you get your washing done.'

His voice was expressionless. I couldn't tell if he believed me or not. I started to get out of the car, cursing lightly as if I'd just grasped how late I was, but he caught my arm, saying, 'Sit down. I'll take you.'

'It doesn't matter,' I said, feeling desperate now. 'I'll run. I'll do the washing later.'

'Sit back, and shut up,' he insisted.

Since it wasn't really going to make any difference, I did what I was told without protesting. He drove fast but carefully enough, and we were there in minutes. I stood on the pavement, waiting to see him safely out of sight. He smiled briefly at me. I realized that he was waiting to see me safely inside the pillared Victorian building. I turned and went up the long flight of steps. There was a group of student types hanging about, finishing their cigarettes or else waiting for friends who hadn't turned up yet. At the door I looked back. The rat was still watching. So I had to go in.

16

Missing the Bruckner

A tall, thin, permed female stopped me a few feet inside the door. She wore a navy and white summer dress in the same style my grandmother liked, discreet frill to hide the sagging neck and rigid pleats down below. With her pearl ear-rings and the half-moon specs on a gilt chain, she could have been any one of Doris' bridge set.

'Good morning,' she said, in a bright official voice, 'Do you have a ticket?' Her eyes took in my hair and my clothes. Her smile became slightly congealed. I'd have turned on my heel, but I was sure McGuigan would still be sitting on that yellow line, watching the door.

I showed her my ticket. She took a hesitant step back to let me pass. I could guess what she was thinking—classical music appeals to such a wide audience nowadays. She twittered anxiously after me, 'You will watch that you don't cause an obstruction, dear? With your rucksack? We have some partially sighted friends...'

Some of the fully-sighted orchestra were already in their places. I looked round. The windows were all stained glass. The place must have been a church. Now it had red plastic seats instead of pews, but it still felt like a church, cold and lifeless, and closed in on itself.

The audience were mostly middle-aged or older, though there were a couple of families with kids and a few groups of students, including the ones from the steps who'd come in close behind me. They all seemed to know one another. There was a lot of squealing and waving and noisy excited shuffling as they tried to get seats close to each other.

I was loitering at the beginning of the right-hand aisle, thinking I'd not bother sitting, because it would be easier to get out in ten minutes or so if I just stood at the back. Unfortunately, a skinny old man with a huge Adam's apple lurched at me and insisted on ushering me to a seat about twenty rows down.

It looked as if all the musicians were in. I caught sight of Colin, but he didn't see me. He was sideways on, deep in discussion with a very pretty red-haired female on his right. I felt a sudden stab of envy. He'd looked ridiculous yesterday in his pink wig. I'd enjoyed feeling sorry for him. Today he was in his own world, and I was the outsider. He looked happy, and sure of himself. He could do something other people paid money to hear. He was part of something important. I was willing to bet his father came home sober every night. His mother probably brought him breakfast in bed. The poor guy had never done me any harm, but right then I almost felt I hated him.

Beside me was a strange-looking male wearing a

kilt. The first real one I'd seen. He had the socks with the knife down the side as well. He wore long side-burns and a massive handlebar moustache, even though he couldn't have been more than maybe twenty five or so. To my surprise, he now pulled out a packet of Polo mints and offered me one. I shook my head.

'Didn't they give you a programme?' he said in a loud whisper. His accent was excruciatingly polite. 'Would you care to borrow mine?'

'I'll just listen,' I told him. 'It's OK.'

A voice said, 'Jon?'

I leaned forward. Two seats along, on the far side of my mint-eater and a massive, red-faced woman in a black jumper, Casey was staring at me.

'What are you doing here?'

Speechless, I stared back at her, my mind a complete blank.

There was a burst of applause. A tall, extremely hairy man came in and sat near the front at the end of the first row of violins.

I leaned forward again. Casey began to say some-thing, but the fat woman shifted in her seat and said, 'Ump hmm,' in such an indignant voice that Casey sat back, quelled.

More applause, this time for two men. One stood back as if to let the shorter one take most of the adoration. Then the whistle went and they were off.

I couldn't think straight. She was surprised to see me. Was she angry, or pleased? I had nothing to go on. I wished I could read minds. She might be thinking I'd come because I liked this kind of music. I couldn't remember if I'd told her I didn't. But Colin had said he was going to the hospital, so he might have told her he'd given me tickets, and that I'd known she was supposed to be here. Which made it look as if I was chasing her. Great.

I suppose the music must have been good, because everyone wore expressions of pleasure and rapt attention. The mint-eater was conducting with one hand, an inch above his knee, nodding his head slightly at what may have been specially good bits. I hadn't a clue what they were playing, except it wasn't the Enigma Variations by Edward Elgar. I would recognize the Enigma Variations played backwards on a pea-shooter. We'd listened to it *ad nauseam* in school in first and second year.

Sometimes the soloist went off on his own and did lots of fancy bits, but mostly they were all playing together. Suddenly there was rapturous applause. I clapped like everyone else. Then one or two people jumped out of their seats and began rushing up the aisles, and there was a buzz of conversation, programmes rustling, chairs scraping. Some of the orchestra were moving about too. The end, or an interval?

I had to get out of my seat to let the mint-eater and the fat woman out. I just kept going. Deliberately not looking towards Casey, I joined the general move towards the rear of the hall. If it hadn't been for the rucksack I'd have made it, but I couldn't edge past people. What I'd been expecting and fearing happened.

'Jon! Jon, wait a minute!'

I tried to ignore her. I didn't want to speak to her. Not here, not with all these people, not with my face messed up. I was feeling distinctly walked over, after the run-in with my father. The session with McGuigan hadn't helped. Basically I was angry at everything, angry at her most of all. I'd stuck by her, helped her, stopped her from panicking... Then after all we'd been though, she'd dropped me like a dirty handkerchief...

She had me by the sleeve.

'What did you do to your mouth?' she wanted to know.

'I walked into a door.'

'It looks really sore.'

'Thanks.'

'Where are you going? What's wrong?' she caught at me again, as I turned away. 'Oh, I'm sorry,' she apologized to a couple with a kid in earnest spectacles, who were trying to get past us. 'This is hopeless,' she said hurriedly, 'Come to the kitchen with me. How did you hear about this concert, anyway?'

'Come where?'

'I'm supposed to be setting out food, so it'll be ready after the second half. But nobody'll mind if you come. Didn't you think of putting ice on it? Come on, we can talk downstairs.'

I didn't move.

'I'm sorry,' she brushed her hair off her face and smiled as if in sudden understanding. 'You don't want to miss the Bruckner.'

'There's nothing to talk about,' I said shortly.

'What d'you mean?'

I hated it when she looked at me like that.

'I'm... I'm going for a train. I don't have any time...'

She looked at me closely.

'Which station?'

'Just the main one.'

'There are two of them. Central or Queen Street?'

'Does it matter?' I said angrily.

'Not if you don't mind whether you're going north or south.'

We stared at each other in silence for several seconds. Then I heard my voice asking, 'What time did you come home last night?' I waited for her to tell me it was none of my business.

'I didn't. I've been at the Cardosis'. She insisted. She wouldn't hear of me staying on my own.'

'So where was Romano?'

'Working. He wasn't going to be back till after midnight, I think. But Bob's getting out this afternoon. He's a lot better. Very grumpy, so he must be better. He phoned us at eight this morning, complaining about the hospital porridge.'

'What was wrong with it?'

'Full of lumps.'

'I never eat it myself,' I said.

'Me neither. I'm basically a cornflakes person.'

'I mostly just have a slice of toast.'

'With marmalade?'

'Or syrup. If there is any.'

'I love syrup, but it's messy.'

'I usually eat it at the sink.'

My anger had gone. It couldn't hold out against her smile. It had slipped silently away, wandered off, like a restless kid bewildered by this crazy conversation. I didn't care what we were talking about, just as long as we could go on talking.

'Are you really going for a train?'

Not if you don't want me to. But I only said it inside my head. She had to make the moves. My ego was as bruised as my mouth. From here on, I was risking nothing.

'There's ice in the fridge downstairs,' she told me.

'It won't do any good now,' I said diffidently, but I followed her out into the entrance hall and down a curving flight of steps into a corridor. We reached a door marked 'Staff Only' just as a warning bell rang.

'You're sure you don't mind missing the Bruckner?' she asked.

'I'm basically an Elgar person,' I assured her.

17

Gloom and doom

'Hope, this is good of you. Colin said you were coming.'

The speaker was a slim, fair-haired woman of around forty, in a white blouse and denim skirt, with a mean-looking knife in one hand and a huge chocolate cake on a plate in the other.

'Aunt Helen, this is Jonathan. He's a friend of Bob's. Since Bob couldn't come . . . I hope you don't mind,' Casey said quickly.

'Of course not. We need all the help we can get.'

She looked me over carefully though, whoever she was. There was a friendly smile, but her eyes were taking detailed notes. She turned to Casey, asking how Bob was, then gave us brief instructions about cutting sandwiches and led us to a trestle table against the far wall. There were five other women in the room, busily unwrapping food and loading trays at a central table. Two men were filling what smelled like pots of coffee, and a couple of boys younger than me were wandering about with boxes and stacks of cups.

Everyone seemed to be talking at once.

'It would be easier to get a caterer,' the woman said, 'but they're so expensive it would defeat the whole purpose. Right, we've got thirty-five minutes,' she checked her watch. 'When you get those piles done, see Frances. She's doing the small cakes.'

'Who was that?' I asked when she'd gone out of earshot.

'Colin's mother. Mrs Jackson. She's chairman of the Support Group this year. The money they make out of this goes into a fund for students at the Academy who're really hard up,' Casey explained. 'So they don't starve in garrets the way they used to. Mind you, Dad says TB is on the increase,' she ended mysteriously.

I didn't get the connection so I let it go.

'I'd forgotten your name was Hope.'

She made a face. 'Mrs Jackson taught me at Sunday School when I was seven, so she remembers. There was another little girl called Joy. We couldn't stand one another. Hey, cut through the middle,' she said hurriedly, as my knife went off course.

'Four triangles the same, or people start whinging. Oh,' she said abruptly, 'I forgot. We were going to put ice on your lip.'

'It's too late now. Anyway, it looks worse than it feels.'

'How did you do it?' she frowned. 'I would have thought your nose would have got there first.'

'It wasn't a door. It was a low-flying signet ring.' I slid my completed pile of quarters to the left and reached for more.

'A what?'

'Nothing,' I said. The last person I wanted raising his ugly presence in this conversation was my father. I trusted he was still insensible. I was safe from him here, and I wasn't going back anyway. What was I going to do? I pushed that question away. Time for that later. Casey was waiting for me to speak. I groped for something interesting and came up with McGuigan.

'That detective was at me this morning, the one with the sandy hair.'

Her eyes widened. 'Why? We told him everything last night.'

'Maybe he didn't believe us.'

'Mr Cardosi said we had nothing to worry about.'

'Good for him,' I said, a little cynically.

'But we didn't actually do anything wrong. They got the money back. It's over.'

'Whose money was it? Does Cardosi know?'

'He sort of hinted. I think it was that cousin Mano told us about, the one who left the country. He was down in London then he came up to Glasgow in a hurry, then he went to Italy. His parents won't have anything to do with him. I think he's been in trouble before, but not as bad as this. Mrs Cardosi says it's all because he went to England. You'd think nobody in Scotland ever broke the law.'

'Maybe that's why McGuigan doesn't like me. I'm a dangerous hard man from the south.'

'You take everything really personally, don't you? I know he was grumpy. But that's his job. And they work terrible hours. I thought he looked exhausted.'

She was at it again, determined to look on the bright side, desperate to find something nice about everybody. I knew McGuigan didn't like me. One glance and he'd pinned a label on me. She'd used the word 'grumpy', but at the time he'd upset her to the point of tears. I was sure she'd been as scared as me. Then I wondered if Casey did it out of self-defence, this cheerful, find-the-silver-lining act. Because if you could convince yourself that danger was a relative thing, and that people who scared you were really not so nasty after all, then you didn't have to be that scared.

Casey could see where Mrs Cardosi was wrong, making out that her nephew was basically a decent lad who'd been led astray by foreigners, but she was doing much the same thing herself. Altering reality to make it easier. I preferred to face the facts. McGuigan had scared me the day before, and I didn't mind admitting that, or the fact that he didn't like me any more than I liked him.

One thing still worried me. He'd said nothing about the wire. The more I thought about it, the less sure I felt that he'd set it up. So who had? Not Romano. His initial shock and concern for Bob had been genuine.

Suddenly it occurred to me that McGuigan might be thinking I'd done it, and that in producing the wire, I'd been trying to work some kind of cover-up. Was that why he'd come back at me so quickly? Romano could have told him about it before I had. Did Romano think I'd done it? I wondered how much Bob had remembered, or whether Romano had mentioned the wire to him. Would Casey know? I tried a kind of indirect approach, in case she still didn't know that the fall hadn't been an accident.

'What did Romano tell Bob?' I said casually.

'When?'

'At the hospital last night. What did he say?'

'He didn't come in.'

'What?'

'He stayed in the car.'

'Why?'

'To let us have some privacy. Anyway, he was eating his fish.'

'So he didn't come in at all?'

'What's wrong with that? He knew I was upset . . .' she paused in her slicing. 'What does that look mean?'

'It doesn't matter.'

'Don't start that again. Tell me what you're thinking.'

I was thinking that I'd been right about Romano Cardosi. I was sure of it now. Sweet-talking Casey and me was one thing, but he was obviously too scared to face Bob. He knew that Bob would see right through him. It looked as if his days in their basement would be numbered. Unless of course my guess was wrong and he had genuinely been thinking of them, and how they might want time alone. I just couldn't bring myself to believe that though.

'Is he the same as you, your brother?'

'In what way?'

I was meaning, was Bob naive, but I stopped myself just in time. There was no way of putting it without getting her back up.

'It doesn't matter,' I said, for the second time in two minutes.

To my surprise, she almost snapped at me. 'I could shake you when you're being like this. You screw up your face and you start asking things and then you clam up like . . .'

'Oh, great, you're almost there.' The blonde woman was at my elbow. 'Right, stack them on these trays and take them upstairs. Frances has finished her lot. I think we're going to do it. Make sure you grab something yourselves before the hordes descend.' Then she said to me, 'Can you eat? We've got some ice-cream for the under tens.'

'I'll be OK.'

'Well, there's some left in the upper part of the freezer if you change your mind.' With that she left us.

No jewellery. Hardly any make-up. Not Doris' type at all. I wondered why Colin hadn't told her what his job was. She didn't look as if she'd mind that much.

'Why hasn't Colin told her about his summer job?' I asked Casey.

'Hasn't he?'

'No. At least, that's what he said last night.'

'Where did you see Colin?'

'I met him in the street. He gave me a ticket for this. Why doesn't he tell them what he's doing?'

'Would you have?'

'I wouldn't have taken the job. But if I had, I'd have been honest about it.'

'Let's get this done,' she said shortly, pushing a tray at me. When everything was loaded she led the way towards a door at the far side of the room.

'If it was me,' I objected, 'I'd have told them. He's pretty stupid if he thought nobody was going to spot him. He's a fool. Somebody should sort him out, take him aside and wise him up on . . .'

'What are you picking on Colin for?'

'I'm not picking on him.'

We were facing each other, loaded trays in our arms, holding a pair of swing doors open with our backs. A short man with an urn staggered through between us and up the long flight of stairs, followed by the two small boys with jugs of milk on wobbling trays.

'You don't like Colin, do you?'

'Not particularly,' I admitted.

'Why not?'

'Why should I?'

'Was he witnessing to you?'

'Was he what?' I looked at her blankly.

'Talking to you about Jesus.'

'No,' I said incredulously. 'Does he do that sort of thing?'

'Of course. I would too, if I thought you'd listen. But I don't think you would. And anyway, you don't know he hasn't told his parents. He just didn't tell Bob, and I don't blame him, because Bob would have been out like a shot with his camera, taking . . .'

'Oh, you never blame anybody, do you?' I cut in.

She opened her mouth then bit back whatever it was she'd been going to say. Without speaking she began to climb the stairs. I followed, cursing myself inwardly.

We had to go on tiptoe and in silence at the top. The dame with the pearls was shushing everyone, making sure no careless word in the corridor spoiled the performance in the hall.

In the room where the lunch was being set out,

Casey met someone she knew, a tall girl with lank brown hair in a pony-tail, wearing a long Indian-type skirt, sandals, and, unbelievably, grey ankle socks. I moved away. Like everybody else, I helped myself to food, taking a plate and a couple of sandwiches and cakes, and a paper cup filled with nameless cola. Chewing was not easy.

It was a mystery to me how anyone like Casey could be so gullible, especially about religion. In fact, it was depressing. I was glad she'd kept off the subject. Not that we'd had many long quiet interludes when she could have got round to it.

I'd had one or two near misses in the past. There was a man in the village when I was younger, a big guy with nothing on the top of his head and a curly beard, as if his toupee had slipped. He'd tried to get me into his football team. He and his wife had this religious meeting in their house and he'd got a team going for the under tens, but you had to go to the Sunday thing as well. Some of my class went, but I never did, because I reckoned it would just be a repeat of school, one more situation where some adult would thrust a book in my hand and make me try to read or sing, while the rest enjoyed the joke.

Our biology teacher was another one. She has a PhD, so you'd think she'd have more sense. She started a discussion group in the school. This time the lure was barbecues and weekends away, and trips to the swimming pool at Sheringham. She's not a bad teacher though, and my marks are OK in biology because you can do a lot with diagrams instead of words. Actually I think she has a soft spot for me, even though I keep saying I'll come to her group and I never do.

Without warning, the big door swung open and people began swarming in. I lost sight of Casey and retreated to a corner. The noise level was terrific, and they were falling on those sandwiches and cakes as if they hadn't eaten for a month and didn't expect to for at least another. Talk about pigs at a trough!

I was watching them all, thinking of nothing, when I saw the impossible. I looked away, then back, unable to believe my eyes, but it was him, not somebody like him, not a trick of the light. It was him. My father, standing just inside the doorway, scanning the crowd. Feeling sick, I moved behind a large woman on my left. What on earth was he doing here?

The answer was obvious, he was looking for me. But how on earth had he known I was here? It was like a nightmare. Like being haunted. I couldn't get out if he stayed where he was—there was only one set of doors. But once the mob had eaten its fill, the crowd would thin out, and he'd spot me . . .

'Are you going to eat that eclair?'

I jumped. Casey, at my elbow. I stared at her and my mind did its folding trick. One word hung in my brain, humming like an angry bee. Doom.

18

A change of plan

Casey peered anxiously at me. 'Are you all right? You look as if you're going to be sick.'

Speechless, I stared back at her.

'Oh, help,' she said worriedly, taking the plate from my unresisting fingers, looking from side to side for the quickest escape route.

'No, I'm not. It's all right. I'm OK.'

'You don't look OK.'

The truth was stranger than anything I could invent.

'I'm in trouble. My father just arrived and I don't want him to see me. He's at the door. Don't look,' I caught her urgently by the shoulder as she began to stand on tiptoe to see.

'Why don't you want to see him?'

'It's a long story. I just don't.'

'You're sure it's him?'

'It must be. Unless he's got a twin. But he couldn't have known I'd be here . . .'

'Where were you supposed to be?'

'Maybe it's not him,' I was talking to myself. 'Maybe I'm just losing my sanity. Maybe this is how it starts.'

'Jon, it's only your father, not King Kong. Why do you . . .?'

'Look, you don't know him. I don't know him either, come to that. It's just an accident of birth. But you wouldn't like him, I guarantee it. Even *you* couldn't find something nice to say about him.'

'Why "even me"?' She bridled and the little nose went up.

'Forget it. What am I going to do?'

Casey moved away, weaving through a cluster of bodies to push herself up on the edge of a table for a couple of seconds, coming down with a bounce. 'There's nobody at the door now,' she announced.

I chewed my lip and instantly regretted it.

'D'you want me to go down and get your bag?' she asked.

'I don't know. No, I'll come with you.'

We reached the door, crossed the entrance way. We were at the head of the steps when he called my name from behind. I froze. I could hear my heart beating in my ears. I told myself this was ridiculous. What was I scared of? He'd surely never dare start anything here. There were people round about us, laughing, slurping at their coffee, greeting old acquaintances. I turned to face him.

'Just exactly what have you been up to?' His tone was icy.

'Listening to music. And making sandwiches.' My voice sounded astonishingly calm. He looked sober enough. He'd shaved and put on a shirt and tie.

Maybe if I kept my cool, nothing would happen.

'Don't be smart with me. You know what I'm talking about. I've had the police at the door...'

'Excuse me, we haven't met, Mr Moore, but I'm the one who was with Jon yesterday, and it wasn't his fault.' Casey, talking at top speed. 'He didn't do anything wrong at all. It was just an accident, and he was trying to help after my brother got hurt, so it wasn't his fault at all. So please don't be angry.'

He stared at her, clearly taken aback. 'Who are you?'

'My name's Hope Bradley,' she smiled and held out her hand, an adult gesture that seemed somehow out of place.

He didn't respond. If anything he looked totally at a loss. The colour seemed to drain from his face. Then his hand came up, and he shook hers, but like an automaton.

'Mr Moore, if you're worried about the police, maybe you should speak to Mr Cardosi. He'd put your mind at rest,' she went on earnestly. 'He knows about these things, and he said there's nothing to worry about, really.'

'Why did you come here, Jonathan?' He was speaking to me, but his eyes never left Casey.

'Somebody gave me a free ticket,' I said cautiously.

There was an uneasy silence for a few moments.

'Well,' Casey said, breaking it, 'I'd probably better be making tracks. I'm going to get Bob,' she said to me. 'All right?'

The big brown eyes said more. Can I go? Are you going to be all right now, with him? Or do you want me to stay? I could read them as clearly as anything, and I felt a sudden quiver of pure happiness. She cared what happened. She cared about me.

'I'll manage,' I said carefully.

'You want to come over tonight? He'll be glad of the company. He was asking about you last night.' Then she added, to my father, 'My brother's been in hospital overnight, after a fall. I have to go and bring him home, since my parents aren't here. Well, I mean I'm going to go in the taxi with him, that is,' she smiled, willing us to smile with her.

'Why don't we give you a lift?'

I stared at my father.

'My car's outside. Which hospital is it? No sense in wasting money on a taxi, since we're all going back to the same street. Jonathan?'

'Um. Well, OK, if that's all right with Casey,' I stumbled, bewildered by this sudden change of behaviour.

'That's very kind of you, Mr Moore. Are you sure you don't mind?'

'The least I can do. You say your parents aren't here? On holiday, are they?'

Casey launched into an explanation. I muttered that I'd get my bag and left them to it.

They were chatting away like old acquaintances when I came back. Unbelievable. The man was actually smiling. For some nameless reason, this worried me slightly. I hadn't seen him smile, ever. Then I reasoned that it was probably simple jealousy on my part. Casey could charm a lame man away from his crutches, just by being herself. There wasn't a devious bone in her body. But if it meant he wasn't going to be mad at me any more, it was all to the good.

'I would have come, last night,' I told her as I put the rucksack beside her on the back seat of the car. 'But I thought . . .'

'What did you think?'

'That you wanted to see him on your own,' I finished lamely.

'You looked so fed up. I thought you wanted to go home.'

'I didn't.'

'You should have said.'

'Next time, read my mind.'

'I wish I could,' she said after a few seconds.

I sat there in the front seat, as we pulled out of the car park, telling myself that everything was going to be all right.

19

Off course

'I confess I'm surprised at your parents, leaving you for so long.'

'Well, Bob's twenty. He's very responsible,' Casey said quickly, in answer to my father. She leaned forward, 'Dad's been wanting to do this for a long time.'

'He's a clever man. Destined to succeed.'

I glanced at him. It seemed a strange thing to say. He caught my eye and smiled.

'I met Mr Bradley in Norwich, years ago. A very clever man. Oh, he wouldn't remember me,' he went on, as Casey, surprised, began to say something. 'We only spoke together once. But I remember him. He's greyer now, I suppose. The price of success. There's always a price to pay.'

Although it was said lightly enough, something seemed to thicken my throat, as if my tongue had slipped backwards. Yet why shouldn't he have met Casey's father? Coincidences happened all the time, and Norwich wasn't a huge place.

'I've not done so well, of course. In fact, I've done rather badly. Classic case of the poor getting nothing, I suppose. Staying alive must count for something. What do you think?'

Casey looked bewildered by his question, as well she might.

'Um, well, yes,' she said hesitantly.

We'd slowed to a halt at traffic lights. When they changed, he drove forward a few yards then put on his left indicator and stopped, causing the driver behind us extreme and loud annoyance.

'Won't be a moment,' he said, getting out and slamming the door.

I twisted round, to see him disappear into a pet shop, of all places.

'What does he need in a pet shop?'

'You don't have a pet?' Casey asked, watching with me.

'Nope.'

'Maybe he's buying you one.'

'Oh, come on. A chemist, I could understand. He must have a cracker of a hangover.'

Casey looked round at me. She focused on my lip then, as if light had dawned, she looked down. Her hair fell forward like a veil.

'What d'you want to do?' I asked her.

'What d'you mean?' she said, without looking up.

'Oh, I don't know,' I said, exasperated. 'I just have a bad feeling about all this.' It was hot inside the car. I wound down my window, but there was no breeze at all, as if the day was holding its breath. The street was treeless and dirty, littered with paper and empty cans. Two starlings were fighting over a scrap of cardboard.

'Has he ... did he ever hit you before?' Her voice was muffled by hair.

'I don't understand what he needs in a pet shop,' I said again, avoiding her question. Everything here was irritating me, the quarrelling birds, the heat, even the scraps of litter ...

'I thought you just meant you didn't get on. Like arguing about your hair or something. Why didn't you tell me?'

'He's coming back,' I warned her. 'You want to think of something and get out?'

'No, I'm staying with you,' she said quickly.

'Why?'

She picked at the worn ridge on the back of the car seat for a moment then said diffidently, 'That's what friends are for.'

'I thought I was Bob's friend.'

She didn't get it.

I explained, 'That's how you introduce me, every time we meet anybody. Like those girls in McDonald's.'

She didn't get a chance to come back at me, because the old man pulled his door open as I finished speaking.

'Sorry about that,' he said cheerfully. 'Just an idea I had.' Something in a brown paper bag rattled like loose change. He wedged it between his side of the dashboard and the front window.

'Hot again, isn't it?' He loosened his tie, tossing it at me. 'Stick that somewhere,' he instructed, starting the car and twisting his head round to watch for a gap.

I pulled down the glove compartment door. There was a bottle inside. Predictable. I shoved the tie on top. As we drove along, I struggled to work out what was the best thing to do. Or did I actually need to do anything? The way he was talking was a bit weird, but he was driving carefully enough. Maybe it was just the hangover talking.

I wondered when he was going to bring up whatever the police had said to him. Was this why I felt so jumpy? Perhaps he was saving it until we were alone. It must, I realized, have been McGuigan who told him where to find me . . .

'That's our church,' Casey said abruptly. I caught sight of a pale yellow stone building down a side street. 'I suppose we'd better phone Mr MacDougall. He's our minister,' she explained.

'Why phone him?' I asked.

'To tell him about Bob. He always likes to visit if somebody . . . Mr Moore, isn't this a kind of long way round?' she interrupted herself. 'Or is this the route you know? It's just that we usually turn up Baker Street,' she ended apologetically.

My father didn't answer.

We passed some more junctions, then Casey leaned forward again. 'I'm sorry, I should have been giving you directions. We've really gone past the best road. You want to go back and turn left at that Clydesdale Bank, the one with the clock.'

'No, I don't think so,' he said flatly.

The man's pig-headedness was unbelievable.

'She knows the route,' I said, trying to keep anger out of my voice. 'I mean, she lives here. Her father works in the place.'

'We're not going to the hospital. Not right away.'

Baffled, I stared at him. What was he playing at?

'Mr Moore, maybe you could stop somewhere along here,' Casey said after a moment's bewildered silence, 'I can walk from here. You see,' she went on awkwardly, 'it's nearly two and that's when I'm supposed to get Bob. I'm sorry if I've messed up your plans . . .' her voice tailed off.

'There's a place,' I said hastily, pointing ahead. 'At that bus-stop.'

He ignored us. We sailed on past the bus-stop. A large sign loomed up. He made a sharp turn to the left, nearly colliding with a small red van. The next moment we were heading back the way we'd come, but on a fast-moving dual carriageway.

I burst out, 'What are you doing? She has to go to the hospital!'

'This goes right back into the city centre,' Casey's voice was shaky. 'We can't get off on this . . .'

'We're not going to the hospital. Hospitals are terrible places. People die there. My wife did. It was quite a long time ago, but I remember it very clearly. Jonathan remembers it too, don't you, son? Your father probably doesn't, Miss Bradley. But he was there, of course. You might say he had the starring role . . .'

20

A prayer in the trenches

'I was still in Mansewood,' he went on, 'but I knew it would only be a few weeks before I was out. The idea didn't come to me then, of course. I'd thought of it on and off over the years. Then there he was, on the screen in front of me ... He's very photogenic, isn't he? I think they call it screen presence.'

It was like listening to a tape with bits missing. I felt increasingly nervous. I didn't know enough about hangovers to know if this was normal. But his driving was getting erratic. A couple of times in the last few minutes, he'd changed lanes without signalling. We'd been lucky not to be hit.

My mouth was as dry as old leather. I was surprised the words came out at all. 'Where are we going?' I asked.

'Everything just seemed to fall into place after that,' he continued, as if he hadn't heard. 'I never expected to find somewhere in the same street. Money was a problem, of course,' he laughed. 'Money's always a problem. But Doris didn't let me down. I've come for a visit, I told her. Come to get to know my boy. Told her I'd planned a holiday, but funds were low. She got the message. Suited her, of course. Got rid of both of us. It wasn't what I'd planned, exactly, having him along. Then I thought, so what, he's my son, he'll understand why I have to do this.'

To do what? What would I understand? And where did Casey's father fit into this? Behind us a lorry flashed his lights and sounded his horn, intent on overtaking. With a sharp movement, we pulled into the nearside lane. I stole a glance at Casey. She was huddled into the seat. Her eyes met mine and I knew she was totally bewildered. But what could I do?

'A decent night's sleep, that's all I really want. All these medicines they give you, none of them do any good at all. I drink too much, that's a bad thing, but you have to do something. I'll give it up, when this is over. I'll be sleeping all right then. That's the main thing.'

He was quiet for a few moments, then abruptly he said, 'I think there's a bottle in the glove compartment, son. Get it out for me, will you?'

'There's nothing there,' I told him.

'There should be. Have a look.'

'What's the point?' I said as lightly as I could. 'You can't drink while you're driving. Wait till we stop.'

'Don't you tell me what to do,' his voice changed. 'Get it when I tell you.'

We were driving past what looked like a park. Flipping open the glove compartment I got hold of the bottle. He held out his hand. Where I got the nerve from I'll never know, but I flung the bottle out of my open window. It cleared the barrier easily and disappeared into dense undergrowth.

He swore angrily and looked back. We made a wild swerve, and the car behind us hooted loudly. Seconds later, they pulled out and overtook. The man in the passenger seat, a tough-looking bald character with no shirt on, lowered his window and yelled his frank opinion of my father's driving. I couldn't see the driver but he sounded equally incensed.

We were beside a slip road. Without warning, suddenly we were on it. Ignoring a red light, we screeched across a junction and turned. He couldn't have had the faintest idea where he was going. I was scared stiff, but part of me was hoping he would actually hit something, just so we'd stop.

Suddenly the car started misfiring. Cursing, he dropped a couple of gears. The noise and jerking got worse. He peered at the dashboard. I looked over. The oil warning light was on. He pulled in to the kerb.

I was out of the car before he could stop me. I pulled the back door open. Casey half fell out and I caught her.

'Where are you going?' he shouted.

'Which way?' I asked Casey urgently. 'Where are we?'

There was nothing near us but rubble-strewn waste ground. Above on our left, grey concrete pillars supported the dual carriageway, rearing like huge marrowbones. To the right, what looked like a factory behind a high metal fence. More buildings in the distance ahead, but no signs of life.

'Never mind, come on. Come on!' I urged her, pulling her away from the car.

His door was opening. I got a firm grip of Casey's hand and began to run. After a few yards, she pulled free, to run faster. I knew we could outrun him. He was middle-aged and hung over. All that bothered me was that we didn't know where we were running to.

We ran till we were out of breath, collapsing on to a low wall beside a tattered billboard. A metal pole beside us could have been a bus-stop long ago in its youth, or maybe just a pole. There was a bad smell like sewage, coming from somewhere. An empty factory stared at us from the opposite side of the road, its windows boarded.

Casey's first panting words were, 'What's wrong with him? Was he drunk? Jon, he scared me.'

'Me too. I don't know. I think he's out of his mind. He nearly killed us on that road,' I replied breathlessly.

'Why was he talking about my Dad?'

'Who knows?'

We sat there in silence for a while. I was desperate for a cold drink. No chance. There was nothing here. Abruptly I cursed myself. I'd left my rucksack in the car . . .

'Jon,' she said with a sudden groan. 'Jon, your mother. Did she die in that accident? I mean, was she dead on arrival, or did they operate?'

At first I didn't get it, then all at once I saw what she was thinking.

'I don't believe it. That's impossible,' I said flatly.

'How did he know I live in the same street as you? I didn't tell him. And he said my Dad was there. He said he had the starring role when your Mum died.'

I knew exactly where she was heading, where she

was trying to drag me, but I couldn't believe it. I dug my heels in. I wanted her to stop. And all the time, I could feel the past tightening round me, like a noose, like a neckchain.

'But your father's in Africa.'

'*He* didn't know that. What did he say, about seeing Dad on TV? It must have been the thing they did about the new laser technique. Where's Mansewood? He said he was in Mansewood.'

'I don't know. What difference does it ...'

'We're wasting time. He could do anything. He could ... We have to get back,' she stood up abruptly.

'Back where? Casey, hold on a minute. What are we actually saying? I mean, think about it. Are we really saying your father operated on my mother nine years ago, and my father is out for revenge? It's impossible. It's stupid. I just can't believe it.'

'Because you don't want to.'

'Because it stinks. It's like something out of a third-rate film.'

'All right, so what's he doing here? You're supposed to be on holiday, right? It's the weirdest holiday I ever heard of. Weren't you listening to him just now?'

'I'm not deaf! You don't have to yell at me!'

'I'll yell if I want to! I was terrified in that car, and you don't even care. I know I'm right. Your father's crazy and he's out to get my Dad. But he can't touch Dad or Mum, so who is he going to hurt? Me, that's who! Me and Bob! And I don't care what you do, I'm not sitting about here so he can get me!'

I caught up with her before she reached the next corner. She burst into tears. I held her by both elbows. She wouldn't look at me.

'Casey, please. OK, maybe you're right. Just don't yell at me. You could be right,' I mumbled brokenly.

'I want to go home,' she wailed. 'I don't want to be here.'

'I shouldn't have let him drive us . . .' I said bleakly after a few moments.

'It's not your fault . . .' she began, then her voice broke up into more sobs and she buried her face in my T-shirt.

I could feel her whole body shaking, and there was nothing I could do to help her. I was scared how near to tears I was myself. I said desperately, 'I don't know how to feel about him, Casey. I can't think straight. I hated him for so long, because he was never there. Then he showed up and he was . . . pathetic. Like he'd lost everything. And then I wanted it to be . . . like I remembered. Because once I'd loved him. I really had, Casey. I thought, that night, before we left, maybe we could still . . .'

I had to stop. I closed my eyes, fighting for control.

'Maybe you're right,' she said tearfully. 'Maybe I'm just thinking all these thoughts and none of it's true. He hasn't hurt us. He hasn't done anything.'

I clung to her words, like a drowning man clinging to a spar. Then the truth hit me like a thundering wave.

Yes, he had. He had done something.

The wire.

I saw it now. He'd set up the wire.

'He's hurt Bob,' I said, my mouth dry as dust.

'He can't have. Bob's still in the hospital.'

'He put him there, Casey.'

She lifted her head off my chest.

'Don't be silly. Bob fell down the steps. You saw him.'

'There was a wire from the bushes to the railings. No, listen to me. First I thought you put it there for a joke. Then I thought it was Romano. But it wasn't. And McGuigan probably thinks it was me.'

'Are you saying it was your father?'

'I know, it's like something a kid would do. But it worked, didn't it? Bob broke his nose, but he could have broken his neck.'

Or it could have been yours, I thought, my stomach chilling. Maybe the same idea occurred to her. 'I'm cold,' she said shakily, detaching herself from me and rubbing her bare arms.

We had been standing in the shade. But I guessed she didn't just mean it physically. She was shivering inside. For herself and for Bob. She and her big brother were close. She liked him, leaned on him, depended on him. I'd brought back all her fears for him, made them worse. At that moment, I'd have cut off my hand if it would have changed things . . .

'What are we going to do, Jon?'

Why I said it, I don't know. 'Well, the troops prayed in the trenches.'

'Don't mock me,' Casey said quietly.

'I'm not mocking you. I don't know what to do.'

'Are you saying I should pray?'

'Not if you have a better idea.'

'You want me to pray aloud?'

'Just do it. Stop messing about.'

So she prayed. It was short and to the point. She asked God to help us get safely home and not let anyone get hurt. Inside my head, I echoed her 'Amen'. Until I met Casey, I'd never given God a thought in my life. I didn't even know if there was a God. But right then, I wanted there to be one, on our side, listening in, ready to leap to our aid.

21

Hot and bothered

Several minutes walking brought us at last to a street with some parked cars at its far end, beside a modern-looking red brick factory building. The first signs of life we'd seen. Everything else had been waste ground and boarded up windows.

'What are we going to say?' Casey asked.

'We don't need to say anything. We just ask if they'll let us use their phone.'

'Have you any money? My shoulder bag's in the car.'

'All right, so we phone somebody and reverse the charges. Whose number do you know?'

'Well, the Jacksons', but there won't be anyone there. If we had money we could phone for a taxi. Then we could...'

'But we don't. Come on, think of somebody else. What about the Cardosis?'

'I'm not even sure of their address.'

'There can't be that many in the phone book.'

'In Glasgow? There's hundreds of them. It's like

Smith or Jones.'

'All right. McGuigan.' It was all I could think of. I rejected the idea that this was betraying my father, because we'd moved on from that scene now. And in a way, McGuigan was exactly the right person to get us out of this. He was partly to blame for getting us into it, if I was right and he'd told my father where to find me.

'Who is McGuigan?' Casey was asking.

'Our pet detective, remember? And dialling 999 is free.'

The red brick building was a builder's merchants. There was a fenced-in yard at the side. We picked our way round heaps of broken piping and piles of wood to a creosoted wooden door with a push-bell, which I pressed.

A male in grubby blue overalls opened the door. He was about twenty or so, but smaller than me. His eyes were too close together and his hair was red and greasy, falling in a middle parting to down below his ears.

'The boss's no back yet,' he said, as if we'd asked a question.

'Can we use your phone?'

'Naw. Ye cannae.' He looked at me in mild astonishment, as if I'd asked to borrow his front teeth.

'It's an emergency,' I told him tersely.

'Big deal. Find a phone box, pal.'

'You don't understand,' Casey butted in. 'We want to dial 999. So it won't cost you anything, and it's really urgent.'

He seemed to see her for the first time.

'Please. It really is an emergency.'

The pleading smile seemed to affect even his minimal brain.

'All right,' he told her grudgingly. 'But he stays outside. You make the call. And don't you touch nothin',' he warned me.

It wasn't till the door fell shut behind them that I thought about the possibilities of this situation. Then I tried the door, tried shoving it with my shoulder, then banging it, tried leaning on the bell. Nothing happened. I wasn't on my own there for more than maybe eight minutes, but it felt like eight hundred and my imagination ran amok the whole time.

When the door opened again, and Casey came out looking untroubled—that is, no more troubled than before—I thought my legs were going to buckle under me. The creep with the red hair wasn't with her. We made our way back out to the street.

'Are you all right?' I asked.

'Well, I didn't know what to say, so I just said we'd been helping Inspector McGuigan yesterday, and now we were in trouble. I didn't get to speak to him, though. I can't believe it. Yesterday we were desperate to get away from him, now we're desperate for him to find us.'

She was incredible. She hadn't a clue about what had been going on in my mind. Fifteen going on five. I didn't understand how anyone so intelligent could be so naive. I tried to pull my thoughts together, but it was like chasing live spaghetti.

'So what did they say?'

'We've to wait here. They're going to send a car.'

'How long till they get here?'

'They didn't say. I am just so thirsty. There's no

shade anywhere here,' she looked round unhappily. 'I wonder what he's doing. Your father, I mean.'

I squatted down on the hot, cracked pavement, without answering. Even the weeds round here looked deprived. They came out with the slightest tug.

I dropped my head on to my arms. I was exhausted. I just wanted this whole nightmare to be over. Like the old song said, you don't know what you've got till it's gone. Life at home, predictable and tedious, all of a sudden seemed to me like a vision of paradise.

'Jon, why did you want me to pray?'

Why had I wanted her to pray? I didn't know. I didn't want to think about it. Silence washed around us, silence and heat. The only sound was the dull hum of traffic very far away. A large grey spider scuttled out of the clump of weeds I was picking at, collided with my trainer, altered course and headed down a nearby crack in the slab.

I thought about Doris some more, remembering what my father had said, and a bad taste gathered in my mouth. It sounded as if she'd given him money, bribed him, more or less, to take me off her hands. The thought of going back made my heart sick. But where else could I go?

'You've never given God a chance, have you?'

She was down beside me on the pavement. I let her talk because I didn't want to argue with her, but I wasn't really listening to what she was saying. I decided maybe she had to get it out of her system. At least that's how it started. Then I found I *was* listening. Which annoyed me, because I had quite enough trouble already.

Then she started getting personal. Personal about herself, that is. About how believing in Jesus had changed her. I'd never been as honest with anybody as she was with me. I couldn't handle it.

'Why are you telling me all this?' I broke in.

'Because I don't want you to . . . to waste your life,' she said after a long pause.

I didn't want to waste it either. But I wasn't convinced that what she was telling me was the answer to all my problems. Nice if it had been, but nothing was that simple. I turned my head to face the other way.

And saw a red car in the distance. Coming fast. My body went cold. He'd got it going somehow. He'd found us . . . But even as I stared in disbelief, I saw, some distance behind it, what looked like a white police car.

22

Blind fight

He drew up next to us. The police car stopped behind him. Casey and I stood there like dummies. Two uniformed men in shirt sleeves got out of the patrol car, putting their hats on, looking round about them as if there was no need for urgency. Which for them there wasn't. My father's face was expressionless. He stared at me through the open window of the car, as if he was trying to read my mind.

'Get in,' he ordered me quietly.

'You must be joking.'

'Get in the car, Jonathan.'

When I didn't react, he came out. Instantly Casey moved behind me, so that I nearly fell over.

'Right then, what's the problem? Who was it phoned us?' It was the older of the two, a thin man with a dark moustache. The other was younger, clean shaven and strongly built.

'I phoned you.' Casey's voice sounded like a child's.

'You shouldn't have done that, Hope,' my father

said hurriedly. 'The car broke down,' he turned to the policemen. 'I knew I could fix it. I'm an engineer, you see. But they wouldn't wait. You really shouldn't have called the police, Hope.'

He put a heavy hand on my shoulder. I pulled away.

'Come on now,' he said, 'This is ridiculous. You can't tell them anything these days, can you?' he said, uniting himself with the policemen, adults against the rising generation. 'The car's perfectly all right now. We'd better be on our . . .'

'Just a minute, sir,' the one with the moustache cut in. 'You do realize dialling 999 without due cause is a serious matter? Are you their father, sir?'

'The boy's my son. I can't apologize enough for this, officer. I'll make sure they don't do it again.'

Once again he tried to get hold of me, my arm this time. I pulled away. My hand accidentally caught the side of his glasses, knocking them off his face. He cursed aloud, lunged at me, and I stepped back. Something cracked under my foot. I looked down. He'd heard the unmistakeable noise too. His mouth opened wide, but no sound came out. I heard one of the policemen say something, then abruptly I was doubled over, as my father's fist caught me hard in the stomach. Gasping for breath, I landed on my knees.

I heard the older policeman exclaim, 'Here, stop this! We don't need this kind of carry on.' Then there was the sound of another blow and he staggered past me. I tried to stand up and fell over. The other policeman was talking fast, warning my father to calm down. I saw the first one put a hand to his nose. Bright blood was gushing from it, splattering his immaculate white shirt.

Then Casey screamed. I whirled round. My father had grabbed her by the arm, was pulling her away from us. He dug in his pocket with his free hand, for something long and dark with a shiny end that caught the light. In a split second he'd jerked her round, and now he had her by the neck, trying to twist something round it. Her fingers clutched wildly, fighting to keep it loose. Her screams stopped as if she'd swallowed them.

Shakily, I got to my feet. At once the young policeman was beside me. 'You keep out of this, son,' he said quietly, barring me with a broad, freckled arm. 'Just keep back. You OK, Andy?' he said, without looking back at his colleague.

'Watch yourself, Alan. I'm OK.'

I could hear the crackle of his radio, and his voice, distorted by the damage to his nose, calling for reinforcements.

'Don't come any closer!' My father warned us.

'That's fine, sir. Just let the lassie go now. We're staying here. You let her come over to us, all right? You don't want to hurt her.'

He peered towards us, half-blind without his glasses.

'I can't let her go,' he said. 'Not now.'

'Yes, you can,' the man beside me urged, his voice gentle as a breeze. 'She's tired. She wants to go home. Just let her . . .'

'No. It's too late. She wants me to do this. She won't let me sleep. I've waited too long already.'

The other policeman was beside us. He was a mess. 'You want to try and get behind him?' he said, through a reddening handkerchief he was holding to his nose.

'Not with that round her neck. It's a blasted dog lead,' the young one muttered back.

Until he grabbed her, it had all been like something in a bad dream. Part of me had still been refusing to accept that he meant to hurt Casey and her family. My head felt as if it was going to explode. I couldn't take any more...

'Wait a minute. Dad.' The last word stuck in my throat. I looked straight at him, trying to blank out Casey's white, terrified face, trying desperately to sound calm. My heart was thumping in my ears. I forced myself to say it again. 'Dad. What about me?' My mouth was drier than a bone.

He looked at me blankly.

'I'll do it for you.' The words came from nowhere. More followed, how I don't know. My voice, but not me at all. 'She was *my* mother. I'll do it for you.'

My legs took me forward. I had no clear idea what I was going to do. He was staring at me, the way he had before. His eyes were lost, old and tired, older than the rest of him. He took a deep breath, as if up till then he hadn't been breathing at all. I sensed rather than saw the dog lead slackening off, and Casey moving slightly. I flung myself at the lower half of his body and we crashed to the ground.

The next moments were a blur of noise and pain. We rolled sideways. I held on. Then the kerb reared up and smashed into my arms, and I had to let go. His knee caught me under the chin. Blindly I tried to get hold of him again, but there were hands dragging us apart, and lots of shouting, and the taste of blood in my mouth, and Casey crying my name.

154

23

Repercussions

The one thing I remember clearly is Casey clinging to me while we waited for the rest of the police to show up, and how it hurt my back and I didn't care. I'd done something right in my life for once, and she was OK, and that was all that mattered.

By the time we'd been to hospital and back to the police station, to wait, and answer questions, and wait some more and answer yet more questions, I'd lost track of the time, and I just felt sick. After they'd finished with me, I didn't even want to talk to Casey. When I thought about what my father had done, what he had tried to do, and how I'd made it easy for him, I felt like a bad taste in my own mouth. I was like something thrown up on the beach that even the crabs would take a detour round.

They weren't happy about letting me go back to the flat to stay on my own. But as McGuigan himself had pointed out earlier, I was sixteen, and legally I was an adult, so they couldn't stop me. His partner the Detective Sergeant and a uniformed constable took me back.

By this time the day was beginning to fade. In the cheap light of the sixty watt bulbs, the place looked worse than it did in daylight. And it stank. When I went through to the kitchen, the bits of glass were still scattered over the carpet beside the sink. I sat down at the table and laid my head on my arms.

I heard the constable call to the CID man after a few minutes, but I didn't pay much attention. In fact I didn't even hear them talking to me at first. They were asking which was my room.

'That one,' I said dully. 'Next to the bathroom.'

'Who used the one opposite the front door?'

'It was my Dad's.'

'You ever use it?'

'No, he kept it locked,' I said, letting my head fall back on the table. I wanted to sleep. I think I was gone for a few minutes, because the next thing I knew one of them was prodding my arm and speaking to me. I mumbled, 'Yes. OK,' which must have been the right answer, because after that they left. I did sleep then, waking with my back cold and my neck stiff.

A bell was ringing and ringing insistently. The door. I stumbled through to the hall and pulled the lever that would let the main door open downstairs. More questions, I thought wearily, waiting in the doorway.

But it wasn't the police. It was Colin.

I tried to shut the door, but he got his weight on it first. 'Hey, let me in,' he exclaimed through the gap, 'I want to talk to you.'

'Leave me alone!'

'This is stupid. Let me in.'

I suggested crudely what he could do with himself. I was scared stiff, guessing at once what he was here for. I think I'd been expecting all along that this would happen, that someone would come and beat me up, except I'd thought it would be Romano.

'What's the matter with you? Bob sent me. He'd have come himself . . .'

'I bet he would,' I blurted out. 'Why can't you leave me alone! It wasn't my fault! I didn't know who she was. You think I'd have let him get within ten miles of her if I'd known who they were?'

He was silent for a few seconds. Then he said quietly, 'Nobody's blaming you, Jon. They asked me to come over to say thank you. For saving her life.'

I must have let go of the door, because Colin pushed it open. He came into the dim hallway, closing the door behind him. I was as tense as an overstretched wire, not really sure if I believed him or not, ready to dodge a fist or a knee.

He looked at me steadily for a while then said, 'Is there somewhere we can sit down?'

In the kitchen I watched him taking in the state of the place. Eventually he turned to me, saying, 'You're not going to stay here?'

'The rent's paid for three weeks.'

'What about your grandparents? Casey said they're in Norfolk. Won't they want you to come straight home?'

'Who knows?' I muttered cynically.

'Haven't you spoken to them?'

I shook my head.

'The police will have, I should think. Maybe they'll come for you. I mean, are they fit enough . . .'

'If I'm lucky they'll send the fare. Anyway, I'm all right here.'

'If you say so,' he said doubtfully.

It was none of his business. I didn't know what was going to happen, but it was nothing to do with him.

'What are you going to live on?'

'I've got enough.'

He pulled open the door of the fridge, studied the contents and made a face. Turning, he leaned back against the worktop and folded his arms.

'You could come back to my place for a while. No, seriously,' he went on, seeing my reaction. 'We've always got some stray body or other. There's plenty of space, and we don't . . .'

'I'm all right,' I repeated, wishing he'd go away and leave me alone. 'I can look after myself.'

'Well, think about it,' he said after a pause. Then he straightened up. 'I suppose I'd better get back.' He glanced round the room, picked up an empty paper bag and wrote something on it. 'Here's our number, if you change your mind.' Then he came over to where I was sitting and held out his hand. 'This is on behalf of the Bradleys. But for me too. Thanks for what you did.'

Almost against my will I took his hand. He didn't let go when he should have, which was really unsettling.

'You know, you're going to have to trust somebody some time in your life,' he said quietly. Then to my relief he let go.

I stayed where I was in the chair, not watching him leave. I sat there for a long time, growing increasingly desperate, wishing I could fall asleep again, my head buzzing with a thousand images, none of which I could get hold of properly. The Bradleys. Doris and Walter. McGuigan. My father. Their faces and voices began circling round and round in my mind, out of control, till I couldn't stand it any longer.

'God!' I screamed abruptly, shoving the chair away. It clattered on to the lino. 'What do you want from me? Haven't you had enough?'

I didn't know what I was doing. I didn't think there was a God but it was as if something inside me wanted to yell and scream at him, to hit back at him for wrecking my life. I went on yelling, flinging curses at the four walls, kicking at the fallen chair. It was a cheap, shoddy thing and one of the legs splintered off. I grabbed at it, turned, raised my arm to fling it at the window, and then, to my horror, I couldn't move. My arm was frozen rigid, as if caught in invisible clamps.

I went hot, then cold with terror. The thought flashed through my mind, 'This is it, this is the end, I'm dying . . .'

I can't explain what happened next. My terror went. As quickly as it had come. I still couldn't move, but it was as if I wasn't really there somehow, and in the same split second, a voice was speaking my name. That was all. Just the one word. And I couldn't have said what that voice was like, but I swear it wasn't in my own head. Then it was like being wrapped round with something warm, and I was leaning back, like I was floating.

I don't know how long I was like that. Seconds or minutes, I don't know. And it wasn't really like that at all. Words are no use. I make it sound as if I was fainting, but I wasn't, because part of me knew exactly where I was all the time.

It gradually faded, and I was still kneeling there, facing the window, the broken chair leg at my side. My face was wet with tears. I don't mind admitting that.

I went through to the bedroom and lay down, shoes and all. I couldn't begin to work out what had happened, but I knew now that there was Somebody there. Logically, I should have been terrified, because this stupendous Fact (which I supposed I had to call 'God') was outside and beyond everything I'd thought or experienced. But all I thought was, 'That's OK.' It sounds banal, but that's how it was. I should have been terrified, but I felt completely safe, and totally peaceful, and before long I drifted off to sleep.

That was how McGuigan found me the next morning. Unwashed and crumpled, but fully dressed. I'd looked out of the window to see who it was. Unfortunately he'd caught sight of me, so I had to open the door.

'Go and put a clean shirt on,' he told me. 'We're goin' out.'

'I haven't had breakfast yet,' I protested. 'Don't you people ever have a day off?'

'This is it. Come on. And give yer face a surprise as well,' he called after me.

'What?'

'Wash it, laddie.'

My heart sank at the prospect of more questions, but I didn't exactly have much choice. I assumed we were going back to the police station, but instead he took me in his car to some park with a long pond in the middle of it, stopping on the way at a corner shop to buy a couple of cheese rolls and a carton of fresh orange juice which he handed to me. We sat on a stone bench in an open-air theatre. The sun was warm on our backs. Nobody else was there except half a dozen kids going round and round, showing off to each other on roller skates, their radio pumping out loud disco music.

I waited for the interrogation to begin, but this time he did most of the talking. He'd been in touch with my grandparents, and from them he'd learned what he now began to tell me. My father hadn't been overseas. He'd been in and out of psychiatric hospitals since my mother's death. My grandparents knew, but it was a deep dark secret. He would get better, be released, hold down a job for a while, then crack up again.

'Why didn't they tell me?' I asked McGuigan, struggling to take it in. All these years, they'd lied to me. Nine years of lies . . .

'Why did they lie to me? Why?'

'You'd better ask them that,' he said unemotionally. 'I've told them I want them up here. They should be arriving tomorrow some time.'

'I don't want to see them.'

'They want to see you.'

'No, they don't. They're only coming because you said to, because it looks bad if they don't. I'm not going back with them. I'm sixteen. They can't make me go back.'

They'd wanted me out of the way. They couldn't complain if I wanted to make it permanent.

Had my father known what he was doing? Was he so crazy in his head that it made sense to him? Things he'd said were coming back to me, and the way he'd looked haunted most of the time. I felt sick that I hadn't realized, hadn't really thought... But Doris and Walter, they were something else. Knowing all the time that he was ill, keeping it from me so completely, actually letting me go with him without telling me...

What were they afraid of? That I'd be ashamed of him? Well OK I was. Crazy or not, what he'd done made me feel dirty and ashamed. But his illness didn't make me ashamed. He hadn't chosen that, hadn't wanted it...

Suddenly I wondered if they'd thought dyslexia was some kind of early warning sign, and that I'd crack up myself if I learned that my father was mentally ill. Were they that stupid?

It couldn't just be that. They'd lied to me from the beginning, but my problems hadn't been labelled till I was well into secondary school. No, it was more likely that they thought telling me the truth would be dangerous. I might tell someone else, say someone at school. Then the Ladies' Bridge Circle would hear of it and cut Doris off for ever.

McGuigan let me follow my own thoughts for several minutes. Then he went on to tell me that my father had admitted setting up the trip wire across the Bradleys' step. He told me also what his partner had found the previous day in my father's room, tucked under the bed in a cardboard box—the beginnings of a bomb. The kind you put under a car, McGuigan said. At this, I think I laughed aloud. Hardly believing he was serious, I asked if it would have worked, expecting him to say of course not.

'He was an electronics engineer, wasn't he?' was his reply.

I couldn't take it in.

'What happens now?' I asked dully, after several moments.

'Hospital. A secure ward.' He pursed his lips, 'If he's found fit to plead, there might be a sentence, but Ah doubt it, no' with his history. But it'll be a long, long time before he gets out.'

'What are his chances?'

McGuigan shrugged his shoulders. 'Ah'm no' a psychiatrist.' He picked at a loose thread on his denims. 'What about you? What are *your* chances?'

I didn't answer. Couldn't. At that moment, I don't know if I even cared what happened to me. I was thinking of him, locked up, under guard, maybe not even understanding that what he'd done was wrong, that his haunted mind made him a danger to others. Then I realized I was seeing the ward where Russell had lived. And died. I looked away quickly, forcing myself to concentrate on the boys with their roller skates.

'If you don't go home, what are you going to do? There's enough lads your age sleepin' rough round here already.'

When I didn't answer, he went on, 'OK, so Ah'm the wrong generation, and Ah'm in the wrong job. You don't have to listen to me. But for what it's worth, nobody's blamin' you, except yourself. Ah've spoken to the brother, and he's no' blamin' you for any of it. And besides, if you think about it, if your father hadn't met her when she was with you...' He straightened up. 'Anyway, it didn't happen. He

163

couldn't let the past go. Don't you make the same mistake, son. Give yourself a break.'

I stared at the concrete between my feet. It wasn't that simple. Even if I could get beyond feeling guilty about what had happened, even if the past could be forgotten, I still had the future to worry about. I didn't know where I was going, in every possible sense.

'Come on, I'll take you back. Ah've got other things to do,' he said finally. Then he did something that surprised me. He pulled out a notepad and scribbled something down, tore out the page and gave it to me. 'That's my home number,' he said brusquely. 'If Ah'm out, the wife's usually in. She'll know where to find me.'

'What are you giving me this for?'

'So I don't ever fall over you dossin' in a back close some dark night, for one thing,' he said, sounding almost angry.

24

Grapes next time

McGuigan delivered me back. I heated a can of beans and made coffee, but when I poured the milk out of the carton it floated in yellow lumps on the top and I nearly threw up. Then I looked round the flat, really looked at it, and couldn't stand the thought of another night there. Colin's scrap of paper caught my eye.

All right, I thought grimly. He suggested it. Let's see if he meant it.

I stuffed my things back into the rucksack, grabbed the piece of paper with the number and left. A few minutes brought me to the main road, and the second person I asked knew where there was a phone box.

It was Mrs Jackson who answered, which took me by surprise, but she knew at once who I was.

'Where are you?' she said. 'What's happened?'

'Is Colin there?' I asked.

'No, he's out being a clown in Sauchiehall Street. He gets back about five. Is something wrong?'

'No, it doesn't matter,' I told her, wishing I'd never started this.

'Colin thought you might phone,' she said. 'Tell me where you are, and I'll come and get you.'

'It's OK,' I mumbled. 'It doesn't really ...'

'Just tell me,' she cut in. 'You're in a call box, aren't you? What street are you on? What's next to you?'

'It's a gun shop,' I said reluctantly. 'I think I'm on Western Road.'

'Great Western Road?'

I said it could be, and she asked if it was near the river and next to a pine furniture store. When I said yes she told me to stay put, she'd be over in fifteen minutes.

I hung up, picked my change out of the slot and went out, wondering what I'd done. I was still wondering when she arrived. When I got into the car, she began, 'Sorry I didn't get a chance to thank you properly yesterday ...'

I tensed. If she was going to talk about Casey, I was getting out.

' ... made just under £850, what with donations and so on, so everyone was delighted. Thanks for your help.'

She meant the concert. I still couldn't think of anything to say to her. Phoning had seemed like a good idea, but now I just felt like a fool.

'The answer's yes,' she said after a couple of seconds.

'What?'

'You look as if you're wondering whether you're doing the right thing. You are. I think it's better for you to get away from that flat even for a day or two. But if you change your mind, we'll bring you back after tea. And at least you can phone your grandparents without having to shove money in every ten seconds.'

'They're coming for me tomorrow,' I told her.

'Well, that's good,' she said, sounding relieved.

'Is it?'

'They surely won't be angry with you . . .'

'They'll be angry at having to come for me. They won't be angry *with* me. They wouldn't be angry if I jumped into that river down there and didn't come up.'

'It can't be that bad, surely.'

Why on earth was I telling her all this? I hardly knew the woman. I decided to shut up. I'd go to their house, let them feed me, let them give me a bed for the night, clean sheets, clean towels, all that stuff, but I'd keep my thoughts to myself.

After a few leading remarks which I pretended not to notice, she gave up digging. The only thing we talked about on the way to their house was cars—theirs was a very old Saab—and after that she left me pretty much on my own. I spent the afternoon lying on my stomach in the garden with my eyes shut and Colin's personal stereo wrapped round my head, avoiding reality.

In the evening, the conversation at the meal table was all pretty general. Mr Jackson had accepted my being there without apparent surprise, as if they really did have waifs and strays all the time. He was a big man, prematurely white-haired, with dark eyebrows that gave you the first, wrong impression that he was fierce. He had a very dry sense of humour though, which took a bit of getting used to. The phone rang at one point, interrupting the meal, and it was someone called Alison wanting to talk to Colin; Mr Jackson commented, 'He'll be with you in a minute, pet, once he gets his bib off.' Colin sighed patiently at this, taking the call in another room, and yelling at his father to get off the line.

Their house was big, but not well-furnished. The carpets were old, and some of their books were stacked on shelves made of planks on bricks. The best piece of furniture in the house was the piano. Everything else was a bit worn. There were framed and unframed photographs of people all over the place, and plants in pots, and a stack of old *National Geographic* magazines in the bathroom, which Doris would have called unhygienic.

Watching TV after the meal, I could hear Colin somewhere practising his violin. After a while he appeared and asked if I wanted to go for a run.

'Run?' I asked dubiously.

'On the bikes. If you feel up to it. I'll use Mum's. There's a decent route up round the reservoir. Some of it's off the road, over the moor.'

It surprised me how quickly we got clear of the city. We did a good half hour, first on the roads, then on a rough track across a moor with some tricky heather roots, before stopping at a cluster of low stone buildings, the headquarters of the Country Park we'd been cycling through.

The evening was warm, with hardly any clouds and no breeze at all. We hadn't seen many people up till now, but this place was busy—lots of parents strolling around with dogs and children, and an ice-cream van doing good business in the car park. Colin bought a couple of cold cans, and we parked ourselves at one of the benches in front of the main building.

'Legs OK?' he said. 'That slope through the wood's a killer.'

I just nodded. I wasn't used to hills, and my arms and my back were still sore from rolling about on the street, but I wasn't about to tell him that. 'Nice bike,' I added, because it was. I appreciated the fact that he'd let me ride it.

We talked bikes for a couple of minutes. Then he complained that his shoulders were sore because of the sandwich board, and that he was going to have permanent ridges in them by the end of the summer.

'Why are you doing it?' I had to ask.

'I couldn't get anything else, and I wasn't going to sit around on my backside for two months. But next year if nothing else turns up, I think I'll try busking. I could probably get a quartet together. And the humiliation of playing to the passing punters would be as nothing compared to what I've gone through this summer,' he concluded, taking another long drink. 'What about you?' he added.

'Me?'

'I mean, what comes next? After you go back to Norfolk. You're still at school aren't you?'

I'd been deliberately blocking out Doris and Walter. Now I could feel my guts going tight when I thought about seeing them. The prospect of going back, of living with them again, was chilling. But what else could I do? I couldn't leave school. I had no qualifications for any kind of job or college. The boatyard was out now that Davie Croft had taken his nephew on full time . . .

'Casey said your best subject was Maths.'

I looked at him in surprise. I couldn't remember telling her that. Then I did. When we'd talked about school that day in the McDonald's . . .

'Is she . . . is she all right?' I said diffidently.

'I think so. Considering. I think she's been sleeping a lot. Bob's face is like something dressed up for Hallowe'en, but apart from that he's OK. You should give them a phone yourself and . . .'

'No,' I said quickly.

'Why not?'

When I didn't reply he changed the subject back to bikes. Then we finished our cans and got moving again. All the way back I was thinking of Casey. I really wanted to see her again. Apart from anything else, she was the one person I might have talked to about what had happened when I tried to smash the window. But I didn't believe she'd want to see me, despite what Colin seemed to think. Too much had been done that couldn't be undone.

I was pretty tired out by the time we got back, so I said I was just going to head for bed, turning down Mrs Jackson's invitation to make myself some toast. I was brushing my teeth when Colin appeared in the open doorway.

'I don't know how you'll feel about this,' he began, 'but since I probably won't see you to say goodbye tomorrow, I wanted to say I'll be praying for you.'

What can you say when someone tells you something like that? It was up to him what he did. I was prepared to accept now that God existed, but that was as far as it went.

I spat toothpaste and straightened. 'It doesn't bother me,' I told him.

He grinned. 'Not that it would make any difference if it did. I just thought you had a right to be warned. Keep in touch, OK?'

I said I'd try. Then as he made to go I said, 'Colin.'

'What?'

'What about Cardosi?'

He looked uncomfortable, as if he didn't really want to talk about him. But I persisted. 'They're not going to let him stay there, are they?'

Colin grimaced slightly. 'That's up to them.'

'But he's crooked.'

'No, he's not,' he said quietly, after a pause. 'He's just been stupid. He knew his cousin Tony was into something shady—I mean the whole family disowned the guy—but Mano thought that if he didn't actually see that money, didn't ask any questions, nobody could blame him for having it. I think Mano's always got what he wanted, just because he's the kind of person he is. Everybody likes him. People like Mano don't... Well, anyway, he's had a scare this time. He's actually pretty shaken, behind the calm front he's putting on.' Then he added, 'Bob wouldn't say much more than that, but I know he doesn't mean to do anything till he's talked it over with his parents.'

After that he said goodnight again and left me to myself. I wasn't all that satisfied with what he'd said, because it still seemed unfair. Then I reminded myself bitterly that life wasn't usually fair anyway. And besides, it was none of my business now. I'd not be seeing any of them again.

The following afternoon Mr and Mrs Jackson both came with me to my grandparents' hotel. Oddly enough, it was one of those I'd passed a couple of times earlier in the week. Inside, it had a fountain and goldfish and about a hundred Japanese tourists sitting patiently on their luggage waiting to go somewhere.

Upstairs in my grandparents' room, the adults found safe things to talk about for a while as adults always do, then Doris looked meaningfully at Walter and Walter stopped rubbing his nose and asked when I'd be ready to come home.

On the way in, Mrs Jackson had asked the same question. By then I'd been feeling so desperate, I'd told them what I'd told McGuigan, that I didn't want to go back at all. They'd been surprised, asking why not. Since it made no difference now, I'd told them, putting it as bluntly as I could without offending them.

At first I hadn't been able to look at either of my grandparents, couldn't meet their eyes. Now I looked at Doris, wondering what she was really thinking. She was giving nothing away. She had all the war-paint on, and the best cream silk blouse and the pearls. Every curl in place. As if nothing had happened. As if nothing had ever happened.

I felt as if I was going to choke. I got up and made for the door. They all called after me, but Mr Jackson was the one who caught me in the corridor.

'I can't do it,' I said desperately, in answer to his plea to come back and calm down. 'They've done nothing but lie to me. I can't do it. They don't want me. They're going through the motions . . .'

He tried to move me. I shook my head, getting more and more worked up. Finally he told me to wait, he'd see what could be done. I asked what that meant. He said just to wait downstairs. Could he trust me to do that? I said OK.

Maybe half an hour later, the Jacksons came out of the lift, by themselves.

'It's up to you,' Mr Jackson began, 'but we've talked it over and if you want, you can stay with us for a while. Call it a breathing space. For everybody. You're on holiday from school for a few more weeks in any case.'

'But you can stay longer, as long as you want,' Mrs Jackson added.

'Don't rush the boy, Helen,' he cautioned her. Then to me he said, 'I didn't intend them to, but your grandparents are prepared to pay for your board and lodging. It's up to you.'

There was no point in asking if they meant it. They weren't the kind of people who said things they didn't mean. But I was scared to say yes, even though it was better than Doris and Walter's.

'Let's give it a try,' Mr Jackson said quietly. So I went with them, back to the car.

As soon as I recognized where we were heading, I said, 'It's all right, I've got all my stuff,' because I assumed we were going back to our flat.

'No, we're just going to make sure Hope and Robert are all right.' Mrs Jackson turned round to reassure me. 'I was running in ever-decreasing circles last week because of the concert . . .'

We parked behind the red Peugeot. Mrs Jackson seemed puzzled when I said I'd stay in the car. She began explaining that it would be all right, this was only a quick visit, so I might as well come in, nobody would mind; but Mr Jackson said very softly, not meaning me to hear, 'Helen, the boy's had enough.'

While I sat there waiting for them to come back, I tried to imagine what they'd be talking about inside the house, but it was easier to fall back into remembering things that had already happened.

Looking over at the flat, I could almost see my father staring out of the window, haunted by the past, torturing himself, calmly laying his insane plans . . . And there was his son, at the next window, ignorant, but smug with it, too tied up in self pity to notice his suffering, too angry at the entire universe, desperate for a chance to prove them all mistaken, desperate to be the hero . . .

I turned, aware of the car door opening, thinking it was the Jacksons.

It was Casey. She didn't look all that great. Her face was pale, and her eyes looked darker than ever. Over faded jeans she was wearing a baggy grey sweatshirt that looked as if it could have been Bob's. Her feet, when I looked down, were bare.

She followed my glance.

'I've no more clean socks,' she said flatly.

'You should wash some.'

'I was waiting till there was a full load. Don't look at them. I hate my toes, they're grotesque.' She came right in, kneeling on the front passenger seat, facing me, with her legs tucked under her, and closed the door. Her hair was crumpled at one side, as if she'd been lying down.

'Why did you stay out here?'

What could I say? The truth, for once?

'I didn't think you'd want to see me.'

'Why not?'

She had a real gift for asking stupid questions. And

for expecting answers.

'Because my father tried to strangle you.'

'That was him, not you.'

'It was my fault he got to you.'

'That's not true, and you know it. Please come in. Bob wants to talk to you.'

When I didn't say anything, she bit her lip and looked away.

'Why do you have to make it so hard?' she said slowly.

'Make what hard?'

'Oh, everything,' she said in exasperation. 'You make everything so difficult.'

'I can't win, can I? First you tell me not to feel guilty, then you tell me everything's my fault. I just can't win.'

'Well, maybe if you want to win sometimes you have to let go of other things,' she said heatedly.

'Like what?'

'Like the big stone wall you carry around with you so nobody can get anywhere near you, or help you, or even know what you're really like.'

She was looking straight at me now, and I felt trapped. For a split second I almost hated her.

'Wow, maybe that's why I'm so tired all the time,' I said jokily.

She let her head fall forward on to the back of the seat. I had the horrible feeling that she was going to start crying.

'Hey,' I said. I lifted a lock of her hair and began twisting it gently round my finger.

'Don't,' she said, pulling away so that it slipped loose.

'Casey,' I began, then faltered.

'What?'

'You . . . you can't take down a wall overnight. Not a big one.'

'You could start. You could take off a brick or two,' she said, her voice muffled by the seat.

There was silence for several seconds, then I swallowed hard.

'Maybe I should come in and see Bob,' I said carefully. 'Except I don't have grapes or anything.'

Casey looked up at me and smiled gravely. 'Bring grapes the next time,' she said.